Viva the Brazos Kid!

Bill Watson is not the luckiest of men. First he finds himself accused of robbery and murder. Then he is kidnapped by the gang who actually committed these crimes and gets framed for a further series of bank raids.

As if that weren't enough, he incurs the hatred and jealousy of the meanest of the bunch and a determined and able lawman is on his track.

It will be a miracle if Bill can escape with his life never mind his liberty. But then nothing is impossible for the man who comes to be known throughout the West under just one legendary name – the Brazos Kid!

Viva the Brazos Kid!

Frank Longfellow

A Black Horse Western

ROBERT HALE · LONDON

ISBN 978-0-7090-8665-9

Robert Hale Limited
Clerkenwell House
Clerkenwell Green
London EC1R 0HT

www.halebooks.com

To Martin – the original 'Kid'

CHAPTER 1

By the time Bill Watson heard the click of a Colt .45 being cocked, it was already too late to do anything about it. Besides, he wasn't even wearing a gun himself – it was over beside his saddle and gear where he'd stowed them the night before on bedding down. Now it was just after dawn and he was making himself an early morning cup of coffee over the freshly invigorated ashes of his campfire when some-one, for some reason, had just got the drop on him.

He sighed wearily, straightened up and turned to face the gunman. He'd been careless – should have been prepared for something like this. But he thought that no one would bother robbing an ordi-nary cowboy camping along the trail. How could anyone possibly know he was carrying a small fortune with him? But then money had a smell all of its own and could be scented by the keen nostrils of thieves for miles around. Bill should have known that was the case and he cursed himself for not being more careful. He should have slept with his goddamned weapon strapped to him – no matter how uncomfortable it was. Now he was paying the price for his lack of foresight. Perhaps even with his own life.

As he faced the direction from which the ominous sound had come he saw a man standing there, gun in hand, looking at him with a hard, hostile stare. For a few seconds the pair regarded each other as two animals might who had suddenly come upon one another in a forest clearing. Bill, for his part, did not relish what he saw. His assailant was a short, grubby-looking gent, with narrow, mean eyes, an unshaven chin and wearing a shirt that had clearly seen better days. But pinned on that disreputable garment was a bright object that brought a flood of relief to the worried cowboy.

'Sheriff,' he said, lowering his hands, which he had instinctively begun to raise. 'Am I glad to see you! I thought you were a bandit out to bushwhack me.'

'I ain't no sheriff,' snapped the other man peevishly. 'This is a deputy's badge. And keep them mitts up, I ain't done with you yet.'

Bill stood stock-still and raised his arms again, but in a more relaxed manner. This was obviously some kind of misunderstanding. The lawman was mistaking him for a criminal he was after. Once things had been explained, all would be fine.

'You can come on out now, Stu,' called out the deputy.

In response to his shout, another man emerged from the brush nearby, clutching a Winchester in a rather awkward fashion. He was an older fellow, better dressed than his companion, with the look of a store-clerk or bank teller about him and seemed completely out of his element in this situation. It was obvious that he had been covering Bill with the rifle the entire time, so it was a good thing that the cowboy had made no effort to resist or escape. At that range even a scared rabbit tenderfoot could hardly miss his shot.

'What'll we do with him, Hal?' he asked nervously.

'You keep a watch on him while I go through his stuff,' ordered Hal.

Without further ado he commenced to rummage among Bill's belongings and before long pulled out a weatherproof pouch. He opened it and produced a thick wad of new banknotes.

'How do you explain this, *hombre*?' he said, waving the bundle triumphantly.

'That's easy,' replied Bill. 'I just sold off a herd of cattle in Denver. I paid off my men and was headed back home. There's a bill of sale in the side-pocket of my saddle-bag if you don't believe me.'

Hal opened the saddle-bag, fished out the relevant document and quickly scanned it before tossing it on to the embers of the campfire. To Bill's horror, it immediately ignited and quickly turned into a blackened crisp.

'Nice try,' Hal jeered with a grim smile. 'But no

phoney receipt's gonna save your hide. We know where that money came from, don't we, Stu?'

Stu seemed every bit as shocked as Bill at his companion's precipitate action. 'Hang on a minute, Hal,' he said uncertainly. 'We can't be sure that we got the right man. Maybe there's something in his story. After all, didn't witnesses say that the robbers were some kind of foreigners?'

'Sure,' said Hal, casting him a contemptuous look. 'And how can they be sure of that when the *hombres* all wore masks? And what's more, are you tellin' me a drifter like this,' he indicated Bill with a scornful jerk of his head, 'came by this heap of money honestly? If you do, you're even dumber than I figured you for.'

Stu peered at their captive dubiously. To be truthful, this man actually looked a good deal more savoury than the seedy deputy who had just insulted him. He seemed like the plain and honest cowpoke he claimed to be, indeed, one of the better sort, with clean if worn clothes and well-cared-for accoutrements. In fact the two men in front of him contrasted greatly as physical specimens, with Hal's unappealing appearance showing up even more clearly in comparison with Bill's sturdy build and handsome, clean-cut features. If anything, an impartial observer would immediately place Bill as a guardian of the law and Hal as its criminal transgressor – not the other way around.

'I think we should let Sheriff Delaney decide that,'

he said eventually with a rare exhibition of resolution and firmness in his voice.

The deputy stared at him in anger, vexed that the other had dared to show some spark in defiance of his usually unquestioned authority. But he saw also a new determination in the eyes of his companion and realized that argument would be of no use. Instead, his cunning brain devised a ruse to get rid of the meddling old fool leaving the prisoner to his tender mercy.

'Maybe you're right,' he generously allowed. 'Maybe we'd better let Delaney handle this. I guess we're just not smart enough to deal with a desperado like this.' He couldn't help adding this last bitter, ironic comment. 'You ride back and fetch the rest of the posse here. I'll look after this prisoner mean-time,' he continued smoothly, as if this was the most logical arrangement in the world.

Stu opened his mouth to protest at this plan, for he didn't really trust his fellow deputy.

'Take my horse, it's faster,' interjected Hal, to fore-stall any possible objections. 'Tell the sheriff what's happened and tell him to get here as soon as he can.'

Stu still hesitated over the proposal. On the one hand he was keen to get out of the vicinity as soon as he could. If Bill really was a member of the bunch of miscreants, there might be others around ready to pounce. And it would give him a rare moment of glory if it was he and he alone who rode in with the exciting news of the arrest of a suspect. For a fleeting moment he would be a hero, the centre of everyone's attention; for a nonentity like him it would be a rare occasion in his humdrum existence.

But, on the other hand, he was wary of Hal's wish to remain with their prisoner. He had qualms about leaving a potentially innocent man in the safekeeping of the unscrupulous deputy, whom he feared and loathed in equal measure.

For a few vital seconds, the battle between self-interest and self-respect raged in his feeble spirit. But the fear of contradicting his volatile and violent companion eventually trumped all other considerations and, not for the first time in his downtrodden life, he opted for the easiest option.

'OK, Hal,' he concurred meekly. 'But you'll look after the prisoner all right, won't you?' he added as a sop to his own beleaguered conscience.

'Sure, I'll look after him,' jeered Hal sarcastically. 'I'll treat him like a prince. Now just you run on, Stu, and tell Sheriff God-Almighty Delaney to get his fat ass here in a hurry or else I'll wrap this whole business up without him.'

The two ushered Bill at gunpoint to a nearby scrub oak where they lashed him securely to its short, robust trunk before Stu mounted his horse and, with a last troubled glance at the captive he was leaving behind to a dubious fate, dug his spurs in and rode off in a cloud of dust.

When he'd got out of sight, Hal turned with an evil eye on Bill, who felt his heart sink as that cold gaze fell upon him, as if a darkness had just descended over him, freezing him to his very bone.

'Jes' you 'n' me now, pardner,' he said with heavy menace. 'And we are gonna have us a little talk. By the time I'm done, you'll be beggin' to tell me where the rest of the money and the other members of your gang are.'

He pulled a large Bowie knife from a scabbard on his belt and ran his finger lovingly along the blade. Its wickedly curving blade must have been nine inches or more, ending in a needle-sharp point and a blood gutter all along its length.

'This here's my favourite hunting-knife,' he remarked in a casual, conversational tone as he examined the edge of his weapon carefully. 'I've used this to skin many a jackrabbit, plenty of deer too. Why, I even skinned me a bear once. But you know what?' He looked up suddenly at his hapless prisoner, his eyes glistening with wicked intent. 'I ain't never skinned me a man. Reckon it can't be too different though. Man's just like a bear with no hair. Right?'

Bill felt a shudder of fear pass through him at this chilling threat. Surely the man was not serious? No one could be so evil and depraved as to contemplate such a horrible act.

But the answer to this lay in the wicked, measuring gaze of the deranged deputy who seemed to be enjoying the terror he had aroused in his proposed victim.

'Yeah,' he continued nonchalantly. 'There's this gal in town, works in the saloon. Me and her are real friendly – if you know what I mean,' he added with a broad wink. 'I reckon I could make a natty little bag for her out of your hide. The sort women use to keep their little knick-knacks in. That should keep her sweet on me. How would you like that, *hombre*? Ending up as a whore's handbag? Why I might even have enough left over to make me a nice pair of riding-gloves.'

Not surprisingly, his torturer's cruel humour failed to raise a smile to Bill's pale lips. Instead he strained desperately at the bonds around his arms in a vain attempt to escape this nightmarish situation in which he had found himself so dramatically plunged. But it was no use. The ropes were expertly and tightly tied in such a fashion that he would never be able to wriggle free.

Hal watched him with an amused expression. 'Struggle all you like, boy,' he commented mockingly. 'But I tied those knots and there ain't no way you're gonna get away. You're all mine now and I'm gonna carve you up like a prize steer. You see, a man got killed tryin' to stop you when your gang were makin' your getaway after that bank robbery you pulled. Maybe you didn't even notice that in the excitement of the shoot-out an' all. But that jasper was my brother. Now it's payback time – and I aim to collect.'

So saying, he advanced on Bill, the knife balanced

in his hand and evil anticipation written on his face. The desperate cowboy closed his eyes in sick despair and braced himself, expecting at any moment to feel the steely touch of the blade upon his body, followed by the inevitable, excruciating wave of pain as it cut into his flesh. But then the unexpected, the miraculous happened.

'*Buenos Dias, señores,* I hope I have not arrived at an inopportune moment,' came a voice from somewhere nearby.

CHAPTER 2

Bill opened his eyes in time to see Hal's jaw drop open in astonishment. Simultaneously both men turned their heads in the direction of the speaker.

Standing just a few paces away was a tall, swarthily handsome man, dressed in the classic manner of a Spanish hidalgo, with a short, tight-fitting jacket and flared trousers lined down either side with silver fasteners. Round his waist he wore a colourful red cummerbund and on his head a broad, flat, black hat, with ornate golden thread sewn around its brim. Despite his colourful appearance though, there was an air about this man of someone who was not to be trifled with as he regarded the pair before him with an expression of wry amusement, while toying idly with a leather riding quirt.

Hal quickly recovered from the initial shock of this interruption. 'This is law business,' he said in a blustering voice, whilst pulling back his vest to reveal the star pinned to his chest. 'I was just interrogatin' this here prisoner. So move on, mister, if you know what's good for you.'

The stranger showed no sign of budging but stood there in the same casual pose. An astute observer, however, might have remarked a slight change in the man's demeanour. He was now flicking the riding quirt against his thigh in a tell-tale sign of suppressed anger, and a certain look of iron had entered his dark brown eyes.

'I see,' he said sardonically. 'Do you usually question suspects at knifepoint . . .' he craned forward to inspect Hal's badge more closely . . . 'Deputy?'

At this calmly delivered slight, Hal lost the little self-control he possessed.

'Now look here, greaser,' he hissed furiously, 'you'd better move on and fast. Otherwise you could end up bein' arrested too and maybe gettin' a dose of the same treatment this *hombre*'s about to get, *comprende*?'

The Mexican said nothing but continued to look at the deputy with a cool, level gaze and a hint of a smile on his lips that no longer had anything friendly about it. When he eventually spoke, his voice had changed too; it seemed to come from some far-distant and not very pleasant place, as if borne on an Arctic wind.

'Do not threaten me, *señor*. I do not like threats. And furthermore, know that Don Alonzo goes where he wants, stays where he wants and leaves when he wants. It is not for riff-raff like you to give orders to a man such as I.'

Under this unbearable goading, Hal snapped and with a mad yell he lunged at the man who had just insulted him. But Don Alonzo was expecting this assault and, with a lightning rapidity astonishing in one who had lately appeared so languid, he stepped to one side and, with an adroit flick of his hand, lashed his quirt across the face of his attacker as he charged by. Hal stumbled to the ground with a yelp of pain and groped his head. He'd been shaken and a little dazed by the blow but quickly sprang to his feet again, knife at the ready to deal deadly vengeance to this impudent interloper who had so grievously interfered in his business.

But the scene that confronted him was very different from what it had been just a few seconds before. Instead of a lone Mexican, there were now four of them standing there in front of him. He shook his spinning head in disbelief. Maybe the injury he'd just received was more serious than he thought and he was now starting to see double, or rather, quadruple. But when he peered again through clearing vision, there were still four olive-skinned strangers standing there – heavily armed and looking at him with unmistakable malice.

Beneath the stern gaze of these desperadoes, the arrogant bully's demeanour crumpled and withered like an autumn leaf before a gale. Bill felt almost sorry for him despite the hazardous uncertainty of his own situation. Perhaps these newcomers meant to kill both of them, take all their goods and move on. After all, that was the classic way of all bandits – steal everything of value and leave no witnesses. And he had no doubt in his mind that these were bandits. For, despite the dandified appearance of their leaders (for, from his bearing, Don Alonzo could only be such), the other men bore all the signs characteristic of that breed. Each carried not only a rifle and sidearm but also had bandoleers of extra ammunition swathed across their chests in criss-cross fashion and belly guns crammed into their belts for added firepower. Moreover their physical aspect gave sign of their profession: heavily whiskered, unkempt, sunburned and scarred, these were the faces of men who spent most of their time outdoors, on the run or engaged in fierce gun-battle. But most of all, it was the eyes that said it all: they were cold, expressionless, devoid of either fear or pity – the eyes of hunters and killers, such as one might often see in wild members of the animal kingdom but rarely in the face of a man.

However, the answer to Bill's agonizing dilemma came within seconds when Don Alonzo issued rapid instructions in Spanish and the bonds that bit so deeply into him were suddenly loosened. Rough but not unkindly hands held him up as he nearly collapsed from the tremendous strain he had recently undergone, whilst a gourd of fresh water was pressed to his parched lips. The instincts of these men – savage, hunted beasts themselves – were to

help another they judged to be in the same predicament.

As regards the hapless deputy, that was a different
matter. He quickly found himself in the same situation as his erstwhile prisoner, tightly pinioned to the
self-same oak with his own rope.

When he'd had a long swallow of water and recovered his voice, Bill asked the obvious question of his
newfound saviour.

'What're you gonna do now, mister?'

Don Alonzo inspected him with a measuring gaze.
Up until now he had paid scant attention to the helpless, mute bystander to all that had just taken place.
His dealings had been with the deputy and, as he had
just been rendered harmless, it was only now that he
could turn his attention to the other man who had
inadvertently fallen into his hands.

'To be frank, *señor,*' he said politely, 'I have no
idea. But tell me first, how do you know this man and
what have you done to cross him?'

'Nothing!' protested Bill vehemently. 'He jumped
me with a buddy just a while ago, made some crazy
accusation about a bank robbery and was about to
torture a false confession out of me when you
happened by.'

'I see,' replied Don Alonzo, stroking his chin
thoughtfully. It was obvious to Bill that all this made
some kind of sense to the Mexican, who evidently
knew more about what was going on than Bill did.

Just then another of the gang came up, excitedly

gesticulating towards a half-opened saddle-bag. Bill's heart sank when he saw this, for it was his own hard-earned cash that was in the bag and he knew that he might as well kiss it goodbye right then.

Don Alonzo pulled out a handful of greenbacks and looked at Bill with a new interest.

'And where did this money come from, my friend?'

Bill shook his head wearily. He realized it would be pointless to lie and would serve no purpose anyway. The money was as good as gone.

'It's mine,' he said with an air of resignation. 'I got it by selling off a herd of beeves.'

Don Alonzo nodded and shoved the notes back into the satchel.

'I believe you,' he said firmly. 'But for the time being, you must entrust it to my safekeeping.'

Bill inclined his head in agreement. He didn't really believe this brigand in fancy duds with such impeccable manners. But he hadn't really a lot of choice in the business. A few minutes earlier he'd been in imminent danger of a slow and painful death. Now he was out of immediate jeopardy – for the time being. For that much, at least, he was grateful. As regards the rest, he would have to wait and see and, if the moment came, seize the opportunity to regain both his liberty and his bankroll. But whether such a moment would ever come remained to be seen.

CHAPTER 3

Don Alonzo turned to his men again and issued more instructions in their native tongue. Immediately they started to get ready to leave. Desperate as his own situation was, Bill could not help sparing a thought for his erstwhile captor.

'What about him?' he asked tentatively, nodding his head in that unfortunate's direction.

By way of an answer, Don Alonzo handed him that self-same Bowie knife that Hal had been about to use on Bill before the fortuitous arrival of the Mexicans.

'You may finish him,' he said simply.

Bill recoiled in horror.

'I won't do that!' he gasped. 'That ain't human!'

Don Alonzo laughed, showing a fine set of pearly teeth.

'I will never understand you gringos,' he said in an amused tone. 'One moment ago this son of a dog was about to cut the living flesh off you just for his own pleasure and now you are unwilling to give him a far more merciful death. Where is the logic of that?'

He turned to one of his band and tossed him the weapon. The man caught it adroitly and a wicked grin creased his ill-favoured face. He needed no further orders on what to do. With a faintly scornful look, Don Alonzo addressed Bill again.

'Juan will take care of this matter. You need concern yourself with it no further. Now, mount your horse. For the time being, you ride with us.'

Reluctantly Bill did as he was told. He wasn't at all happy with the way the situation was developing. His fate at the hands of these desperadoes might not be much better than the one he had just so narrowly escaped. But the smart thing was to pretend to play along until the opportunity came to turn things around. Until then he could only watch and wait.

The outlaw chief beckoned him to fall in behind his lead while the others followed after. There seemed little chance of making a break in these circumstances. As regards the fourth bandit – the one called Juan – he stayed back and stood guard over Hal, making a great show of cleaning his filthy fingernails with the latter's knife. The last Bill saw of the wretched deputy was the sight of his face, ghastly and claylike, staring fixedly at the instrument of his own impending execution. It was fitting that he was going to meet the same end that he had been so eager to dispense to Bill, yet the cowboy drew no satisfaction from the ironic justice of it. But he was in no position to do anything about it and so just rode away, to leave the miscreant to his fate.

The little group had not got far before a piercing scream rent the air. This was no surprise for the horsemen, who trotted on without breaking pace. Only Bill started at the sound and twisted around to look back. There was little doubt over what had happened, and a short while later Juan rejoined them, whistling lightly and with the demeanour of a man going about his innocent, everyday business. But Bill knew otherwise and worried that when the sheriff eventually came, it would be him who would get the blame for the murder. And that on top of another killing and the trifling affair of a bank robbery. He slumped disconsolately in the saddle. Regardless of how you examined it, things were going downhill very rapidly and could hardly get any worse. Or could they?

Nehemiah Delaney's face was a mask of impassivity as he regarded the scene before him. As an old hand of the Indian Wars, he'd seen similar sights and a good deal worse in his time. But he'd learnt long ago to hide the anger and revulsion that sprang up from deep within and threatened to overwhelm him as he assumed that air of professional detachment he considered an integral part of his job.

But for the others, there was no disguising the horror they felt; a few hastily dismounted from their ponies to disappear into some nearby bushes from which the sound of violent retching could soon be heard.

Delaney leaned forward in his saddle and studied the grisly corpse of his former deputy, Hal Jenkins.

'Throat's been cut from ear to ear,' he announced somewhat unnecessarily, since the gash was so deep that the man's head had almost been severed. He cast an eye skyward.

'Not so long ago, either. No buzzards around yet.' The sheriff gingerly eased his bulky weight down off his horse and approached closer. 'Crows ain't had his eyes yet either,' he observed laconically.

That was enough to send the remaining men in his posse scurrying towards the undergrowth with their hats pressed precipitately against their mouths.

The oldster massaged his unshaven chin in thought. 'You say you left the prisoner securely tied up, Stu?' The question was directed towards Hal's erstwhile companion.

'Yessir!' replied Stu, looking frightened and sickened in equal measure. 'Checked the knots myself, no way he could have escaped.' The timid deputy feared being blamed for this gruesome turn of events. But Delaney had already moved away, and was scanning the surrounding area.

'There's sign of other riders here,' he announced at length. 'Maybe up to four or five. Must have been the rest of the gang showed up. Guess it just wasn't Hal's lucky day.'

He cast a glance at the dead body with a mixture of pity and disgust. To tell the truth, he couldn't stand the man when he was alive. That was why he'd sent him off scouting in the direction he thought the bandits were least likely to take. And that was why he'd also dispatched Stu Harker, whom he'd figured to be the greatest liability in case they ever did get into a shoot-out with their quarry. But things had turned out differently from how he had expected. And now a man was dead – his head lolling from his shoulders at a grotesque, impossible angle and his shirt and trousers soaked through with his own blood.

'Cut him down, fellas,' he said, with something like compassion in his voice. 'And break out a few shovels – we'll bury him here before he starts to rot.'

'Aint we goin' after the *hombres* that did this?' asked one of the posse, anger and indignation in his tone.

The sheriff took off his hat, looked up at the sun and wiped the sweat off his forehead before setting it back on his bald pate.

'It's gettin' toward noon,' he remarked wearily. 'We've just wore out the horses in the rush to get here. They need rest, shade and water. And so do we. 'Sides, I'm hungry and want to eat. We'll move on in a few hours when it's cooler and make up for lost time then.'

The other men looked at each other. The lawman presented a sorry spectacle. He was old, had lost all his hair and not a few of his teeth and was badly overweight; but what he said still made good sense and the way he spoke made it plain that he would not suffer any questioning of his authority. It was easy to forget the limitations of humans and animals in the excitement of pursuit and the thirst for vengeance. But Delaney never lost sight of what it took to get to their ultimate goal. That was why he was the leader and they were merely followers. With unspoken, unanimous consent they all set about carrying out his orders and a kind of calm purpose settled once more over the little group that had been so badly rocked by the shocking nature of recent events.

Besides, things were a lot clearer now. Instead of chasing around in the wilderness, they had a fresh trail to follow. They were a dozen and the ones they were after seemed to be only half that number. With a bit of luck they'd catch up with the gang in a day or so, retrieve the missing bank money and – depending on how matters went – return home, with or without prisoners, as conquering heroes. It all seemed so simple and straightforward now. Little did they know that this was the beginning of an odyssey that would take them to the far end of Texas and beyond in the quest for a phantom outlaw who would constantly slip through their questing grasp. A man seemingly endowed with nine lives, mysterious, elusive and, apparently, untouchable. A man whose real identity would never be discovered but who came to be known to them and, indeed to history, under one simple, colourful and mythic title – the Brazos Kid.

CHAPTER 4

Bill and his entourage of captors plodded on relent-
lessly for several hours. No words were spoken by
anyone but, from the urgent pace of their journey,
Bill surmised that they were either trying to get away
from what was behind them – which was understand-
able – or forge ahead toward some previously
arranged rendezvous. The latter turned out to be the
answer when, towards sunset, Don Alonzo suddenly
broke from the trail and made for a large group of
rocks off in the distance. He disappeared into them
and, following with the rest, Bill found himself in a
natural amphitheatre of grassy sward, surrounded on
all sides by the grey mass of heaped boulders. It was
a sort of hideout and formidable fortress in one and
Bill could see that the bandit chief picked his dens
with care. Don Alonzo was scanning the area expectantly and seemed disappointed and somewhat
annoyed to find it empty. He swivelled round in the
saddle and gave a swift word of command, where-

upon everyone dismounted. Evidently they were to camp here for the night.

Bill got down stiffly from his horse. It had been a long, hard ride, especially since the Mexicans had bound him to discourage any escape attempt. He held his tied hands up hopefully towards Don Alonzo, who shook his head firmly.

'We will loose your bonds later, when we eat. Meantime make yourself at home as best you can. Juan will help you.'

Bill divined that Juan had been appointed as a sort of guardian to him, for the bandit's eyes rarely left him. This was not a comfortable feeling for the cowboy in the light of that gent's recent, bloody deeds. He felt that the Mexican would just as soon dispatch him in the same fashion as he had done away with Hal. But, for the moment, Bill guessed he was safe and so he set about the humdrum task of sorting out his gear and setting up a rough bed for the night as best he could. Then he settled down to watch the others as they prepared a meal of tacos and red beans flavoured with bitter chilli. Eventually, he was untied and a wooden platter of food thrust into his hands. Simple as this fare was, it tasted good after a long and taxing day. Even the strong, black coffee that it was washed down with could not prevent Bill from feeling sleepy after wolfing his meal. He rested his head on his saddle and looked out over the camp settling in for the night. He knew that he should be looking out for the first chance to get away but his hands had now been secured again, Alonzo was still watching him and the chances of an escape seemed slim to none.

As darkness fell a big moon came up, and one of the Mexicans produced a guitar and began to finger a soft tune. Around the flickering campfire the other outlaws squatted, speaking in low, guttural Spanish, their conversation interrupted now and again by raucous laughter. But neither these sounds nor worry about his uncertain predicament could prevent Bill from soon falling into a deep sleep. His exhausted body demanded respite from its recent trials; it was essential for him to rest and husband his strength for the struggle that lay ahead. For there was no doubt in his mind that this was just the beginning of his troubles and that tomorrow would bring fresh challenges to his existence. But he would deal with them as they arose. The most important thing now was that he was still alive – for the time being.

Only one thing disturbed the tranquillity of Bill's sleep that night. He was suddenly awakened by the sound of arguing voices. At first, convinced that it was some sort of bad dream, he rolled over and snuggled down again, trying to make himself comfortable despite the awkwardness of lying with his hands bound together. But the noise persisted, indeed grew more quarrelsome. Frustrated in his attempts to nod off again, Bill sat up and looked groggily around him. The campfire had died down considerably now and its fading embers cast only a fitful, ghostly light upon the scene before his eyes. Nearby lay the vague shapes of supine figures – evidently all the members of the gang had retired for the night. From one or two came the distinct and unmusical rasp of heavy snoring, but this was not the disturbance that had aroused him. Screwing his eyes into the darkness, he could just about make out the shape of three figures right at the edge of the pale glow of light. One had the tall, erect bearing of a nobleman – it was unmistakably Don Alonzo. He appeared to be remonstrating with a smaller, slighter but no less haughty person, who seemed to be far from intimidated by him, indeed was evidently responding to the stern scolding of the angry hidalgo with no less spirit. Hovering nearby this squabbling couple, but taking no part in the row, was a strange, hulking figure who appeared to be looking from one to the other in bemusement but was being equally ignored by both. The sight was so strange and surreal, as though it were in some fantastical painting, that Bill felt he was having some sort of nightmare. He was about to pinch himself to see if it were all true when he heard a faint snicker of laughter behind him. Turning, he beheld the sinister, smiling face of Juan, who was eying him closely whilst cleaning out his fingernails with the large Bowie knife he had confiscated from his last victim. The grinning bandit said nothing but that just made Bill feel all the more nervous. It seemed that this cold-blooded assassin was watching him day and night and was merely waiting for an excuse to plunge the wicked-looking weapon he was toying with into Bill's heart! The cowpoke thought it wise to settle down and pretend to go to sleep again in case his wary guard should mistake his restiveness as preparation for some sort of escape attempt. The quarrel appeared to have died down now and peace had settled anew in the outlaw camp.

Drowsiness stole over Bill once more but a detail of this latest incident still buzzed around his head like a troublesome blowfly. There was something unusual about the person who had squared up so gamely to Don Alonzo's arrogant hectoring, something that fitted ill with this wild place and these desperate men. With a start, he suddenly realized what it was. The new arrival was a woman, and what was more, probably quite a beautiful one! What the devil was she doing here and what was her relationship with these Mexican miscreants? The questions were resounding around his vexed mind when he dropped off once more into an uneasy slumber.

The next day Bill awoke with a start. All the events of the previous night had been milling around his head and produced a restless and tormented night for him. Had he imagined everything after all? In his present unquiet state of mind, when his very life hung only on the whim of an outlaw bunch of desperadoes, that was a real possibility. But when he glanced towards the newly invigorated early-morning campfire, he immediately saw the unmistakeably feminine figure of the latest arrival bent over a battered coffee pot. The woman was dressed in a short riding jacket and a split, culottes-style skirt from which emerged elegant, highly polished leather boots. On her head she wore the distinctive wide and flat-brimmed hat of a Spanish grandee, from beneath which cascaded a mass of jet-black curls. The clothes were entirely practical and appropriate for an outdoor life on the range, but so well and cunningly cut as to accentuate rather than hide her many female charms.

Sensing his gaze on her, she suddenly looked up and their eyes met for a few seconds. But then she returned to her mundane chore of coffee making with not the slightest sign of surprise or other reaction. Obviously Don Alonzo had alerted her to the presence of a gringo prisoner in their midst – perhaps this had even been the source of their disagreement – and she was treating him with the same indifference as she did all the men in her life: as if he was part of the natural scenery, like a rock or a tree, and not worthy of any notice beyond that.

Bill suddenly remembered the other vision he had had during the previous night – a considerably less pleasant one, and he turned to behold Juan lounging nearby in exactly the same position as before, still meticulously working at his fingernails with that over-sized pig-sticker. Did the man ever sleep? Bill wondered. And how come his nails never got clean?

He opened his mouth to frame a question about the beauteous newcomer to the camp but then remembered that, according to Alonzo, his guard could speak no English. Probably that was one of the reasons he had been picked for the job. It would be impossible to bribe or suborn a man who didn't speak the same language. Nor could any kind of understanding or sympathy easily spring up between two men who could not communicate in even the most basic way. Not that much sympathy might be expected from a man of Juan's bloodthirsty disposition anyway. Moreover, his fidelity to his leader seemed absolute in its devotion. But there had to be some way to escape his basilisk-like vigilance and if that could happen, if only for few seconds, there might be some chance of escape.

But such thoughts were a luxury at this moment; there were other, more urgent concerns to be taken care of. The smell of freshly made coffee wafted tantalizingly towards him and his belly gave a rumble of complaint about lack of recent feeding. He gestured at Juan, who untied his feet but shook his head when the cowboy proffered his bound hands. It looked as though he would have to eat with his wrists securely fastened. Bill rose stiffly, hobbled to the fire and lifted a blackened tin coffee mug. He held it imploringly towards the *señorita*, who was now busying herself with cooking a pot of oatmeal. Without even looking at him, she poured him a shot of coffee and spooned a ladle of the porridge into a simple wooden platter. Bill took a swallow of the hot liquid, all the while fixing his gaze on his surly hostess. The coffee tasted good and the woman looked even better close up than she did from afar, which was the reverse of what was usually the case. She still did not deign to return his stare, so he muttered a thanks and took his food and drink back to his resting-place. It was awkward eating whilst tied up but he managed somehow and after he had finished his simple breakfast, he sat back and relaxed, a rather more contented man. He'd just started the day with a square meal served out by a pretty woman. What more could a man want? Apart from his liberty and the removal of the threat of imminent death, of course. The answer came from the unlikeliest quarter, as Juan thrust a cigarette, which he had previously fashioned and lit, between his captive's lips. With a surprised and grateful nod, Bill took a long and luxurious drag of his first and probably only smoke of the day. Perhaps Juan wasn't so bad after all, or perhaps this was the equivalent of a condemned man's final wish. Either way, he would enjoy the moment and not worry too much right now about the future; it might just be the best way to survive.

Others in the camp began to stir and before long Don Alonzo himself appeared, swallowed a hasty meal and immediately began urging his men to get their gear together and get under way. He was obviously keen to be on the trail, which was wise since yet another murder had been added to the gang's tally of corpses and a vengeful posse had to be somewhere in the offing.

Last to show up was the squat, nightmarish figure Bill had half-glimpsed in the shadows the night before. In daytime he did not seem quite as menacing as in the flickering, ghostly light of a dying fire, but he was still a formidable-looking presence. He was not tall but stood, or rather slouched, some five and a half feet, This lack of height was more than compensated for by an unusually brawny physique, with a barrel-like chest and long, powerful arms ending in battering-ram fists. He was the sort of man you wouldn't want to tangle with in a fight, reflected Bill thoughtfully, and one he would be careful to stay well clear of. He could not see the man's face clearly beneath the shade of his wide sombrero, but he got the impression of a pair of savagely glimmering eyes set under thick, beetling eyebrows, reinforcing his strong impression of some sort of wild creature in human form, a kind of crossbreed between man and beast.

And his attendance upon the woman in their midst was certainly animal-like in its fawning devotion. He watched her as closely as a dog might a beloved mistress, anticipating her every wish and rushing to fulfil it. She, for her part, seemed to regard this as her right and due, treating him with tolerant kindness, as one might an over-eager pet; but underlying her manner there seemed to be a barely hidden air of annoyance and contempt at his clumsy attempts to win her favour.

When he was satisfied that his men were making good progress in getting ready to go, Don Alonzo took the time to stroll over to his captive to enquire solicitously if he had passed a comfortable night, as if Bill were an honoured guest instead of an unwilling captive. The cowboy could have made any of several ironic replies to this disingenuous query but instead he only offered the obvious comment. 'I would have slept a lot better without being tied up hand and foot.'

Don Alonzo gave an elegant shrug of his shoulders.

'I regret, *señor*, that until I decide what to do with you . . .'

Bill seized his chance and decided to take the bull by the horns. It was a risky strategy and might incur the brigand's potentially deadly wrath, but for his own sanity he had to know the truth.

'Are you gonna kill me? If it's all the same to you, I'd like to know one way or tuther, it's this uncertainty that's eatin' me up.'

The outlaw looked genuinely shocked.

'I assure you, my friend, that Don Alonzo is no slayer of innocents. It's true that if someone is trying to kill me, I will not hesitate to do the same to him. Or, if it is someone richly deserving of death, like that vile deputy, I will also gladly oblige. But you have committed no hurt against me nor are you any immediate threat to me. You were merely in the wrong place at the wrong time. But you can identify and describe me to the authorities and at this time I cannot risk that. At some future date, when I can safely do so, I intend to release you. But meantime, do not mistake my humanity for weakness. Should you try to escape, Juan here,' he indicated his hench-man with a jerk of his head, 'will have no compunc-tion in dealing out the same fate to you as he did to that unhappy lawman.'

Bill nodded his head in understanding. He didn't really know how much Alonzo's word was worth, but he believed him about what would happen if he tried to get away. As the hidalgo turned on his heel to return to his men, Bill ventured to pose one last question. It had nothing to do with his survival but sprang from an instinct almost as primeval and deep-seated – that of curiosity.

'Say, who's the woman that arrived last night?'

Don Alonzo turned, an amused glint in his eye. 'Her name is Isabella. She interests you, *señor*?'

Unaccountably Bill felt himself go red, like an awkward schoolboy.

'Everything around here interests me,' he replied defensively, 'seeing how my life might depend upon it.'

Don Alonzo was suddenly brisk and businesslike again, with one of his sudden transitions of mood.

'The woman does not concern you, my friend. And if you are hoping to gain her sympathy or pity for your situation, forget about it. I know her well and her heart is harder than that of my toughest *vaquero*. Avoid her if you can, which should be easy, for she will certainly avoid you. And, above all, do not annoy her with your attentions when *El Bruto* is around. He is her devoted servant and would readily kill any man at a nod from her.'

With these grim words of advice, he returned to his task and, under his relentless goading, it wasn't long before everyone was packed up and they were back on the trail again. As usual Don Alonzo led the way, with the woman and her constant companion following closely behind. The rest of the gang were strung out behind them, with Bill and his guard Juan bringing up the rear, the cautious Mexican always making sure to keep behind his prisoner.

As they travelled along, Bill could not help mulling over Don Alonzo's mysterious warning about Isabella. Was this a jealous man trying to scare off a potential rival? The idea seemed laughable given his present position of utter powerlessness and humiliation. However, maybe their relationship was a little rocky at the moment, given the row between them he had witnessed earlier. Or perhaps Don Alonzo was being genuine in his counsel, perhaps this woman really was dangerous and to be treated with great caution. In her country and among her class, even the most trifling word or gesture could be perceived as an insult to honour, and his safety here was tenuous enough without risking it further through an unwise attempt to engage this female in any sort of communication.

And then there was the man Don Alonzo called *El Bruto*. The name said it all for it meant pretty much in English what it sounded like in Spanish and seemed very apt for someone of his savage, animal-like appearance. Don Alonzo had described him as a sort of servant, but Bill reckoned he was more in the nature of a devoted slave. He watched over his mistress like a hawk and there was no doubt in his mind that the outlaw chief spoke the truth when he said that he would do anything she asked of him without hesitation – including murder.

No, his best plan would be to treat her as she treated him: as if she didn't exist. But she *did* exist, and in a very alluring form; would he be able to help even looking at such a vision of loveliness? Only time would tell, but if he were a betting man, he wouldn't have put good money on it. It was about the same odds as he would put on his own survival, which, on present showing, was a very long shot indeed!

CHAPTER 5

The ashes of the fire left behind by Don Alonzo and his band were still warm when Delaney and his men came upon them. Concealed from sight though the campsite was, it was no mere chance that the posse happened to find it. Being an experienced Indian fighter, Delaney had gained a good working knowledge of how to read sign, but he knew that no white man could ever hope to rival a pure-born brave in that skill. To that end he had made sure to hire a man from the nearby reservation and paid him well for his services in helping track down the desperadoes they were seeking. The fellow went by his given name of Isaiah but was known to all and sundry by his native name of Yellow Dog. He was a slight and sleepy-eyed individual, whose scrawny frame was clad in shabby buckskin. His dark-skinned face was narrow and creased, with a beaky nose and lank, greasy hair from which protruded what was presumably an eagle feather, though in truth it was so old and tattered that it would be impossible to say what species of bird it might once have belonged to.

Despite his unkempt and pitiful appearance, Delaney put implicit faith in his tracker. He had used Yellow Dog before and knew that no bloodhound was surer to find his quarry than this sorry-looking Indian. For a few moments the man wandered around the blackened site of the extinct fire, his eyes reading the story that the innumerable prints and scuffmarks told him. Eventually he returned to his employer to make his report.

'I see sign of seven riders,' he said. 'They leave four hours ago, maybe five.'

The sheriff put his hand to his chin and rubbed his unshaven cheek.

'So they got seven men, we got twelve. That means we outnumber them nearly two to one. Shouldn't be too hard for us to get the better of them.'

The men looked at each other uncertainly. Despite the proclaimed confidence of their leader, the others in the group were feeling a good deal less sanguine about their chances. After all, they were mostly just ordinary ranch hands and tradesmen. What they were up against were bloodthirsty and ruthless killers – they'd shown that by the savage and merciless way they had dealt with Hal Jenkins. Now that their wrath over their erstwhile colleague had died down, wiser counsel whispered in their ears not to end up the same way he did. Besides, they remembered now that they'd never particularly liked the man anyway.

Yellow Dog broke the heavy silence. 'Not seven men,' he proclaimed matter-of-factly. 'Six men, one woman.'

Without waiting to see the effect of this revelation, he mounted his pony and set off at a steady trot to scout ahead.

The rest of the posse stared at one another in astonishment. A woman out here in this wilderness? And with these cut-throats? What were they to make of that? 'That Injun must be on the firewater again,' ventured one at last.

Delaney gave him a withering glance. 'You know as well as I do that Yellow Dog never drinks on the job, though I allow he makes up for it when he ain't. No, if he says that a woman's been here, then that's the gospel truth. Question is, what's she doing here: does she belong to the gang or is it some innocent girl they've kidnapped?'

'Why would they do that?' asked Stu, perplexedly. The timid clerk had little knowledge of the ways of the world.

The sheriff cast him a pitying look. 'Use your imagination.'

Stu turned a scarlet hue as the import of Delaney's retort sunk in with him.

'Oh,' he muttered. 'Didn't think of that.'

Some of the others smirked at their simple companion's lack of common sense, but the more sober among them seemed all the graver and a fresh suffusion of iron entered their expressions. If these ruffians were abusing some defenceless woman, they would be made to pay for it and soon. Delaney belonged to this latter category and so it was with renewed determination and doggedness that he gave the order:

'OK men, let's go get those sons-of-bitches!'

Just as the fox knows when the hounds have his scent, so Don Alonzo realized that his pursuers must be very close behind him. But he was as wily as any wild beast and wasn't about to be caught that easily. As they passed through a narrow canyon along their route, he scanned the rocky cliffs on either side of the track keenly.

'This is a good place,' he announced to no one in particular. 'Jose, Manuel, get your rifles and follow me.'

The two men he summoned duly drew their carbines from leather pouches and went off with their boss. Bill could see the bandit chief urgently conferring with his henchmen whilst gesticulating towards the upper reaches of the heights around them. Jose and Manuel nodded vigorously in response to Don Alonzo's urgings. It was evident that they approved heartily of whatever their leader was proposing. As for Bill, he felt sick to his stomach at the sight of this. It was obvious that these ruthless outlaws were planning some sort of ambush. In such a confined space, if these men were handy with their firearms – and they looked like they were – it could only be a massacre. Men would be shot out of their saddles before they even had a chance to respond. But there was nothing the cowboy could do about it, and that fact made him feel even worse.

With an encouraging slap on the back, Don Alonzo sent his men eagerly on their way. It was evident that they relished the devil's work they were about to undertake, but Bill could not help wondering how Don Alonzo, who had evidently had a good upbringing and seemed to have some finer feelings still despite the brutal way of life he had chosen, could so callously go about planning the deaths of his fellow creatures.

'Gettin' ready for some more killin'?' he couldn't help remarking bitterly as the nobleman rode past.

Don Alonzo reined his horse to a hasty halt and gave him a hard look. Fury entered his eyes and for a moment it looked like as though he was about to vent his wrath on his impudent captive. But with an effort he managed to control himself and his words, when they came, were measured and controlled.

'Yes, my friend, and I will kill as many as it takes to ensure my freedom. I do not enjoy it, despite what you may think, but in life some things are necessary, if not always pleasant.'

So saying, he gave his horse a sharp jab of the spurs and galloped off in a cloud of dust.

'It's not what you think, *señor*. Your humanity does you credit but, believe me, no lives will be lost needlessly. Alonzo merely wants to slow down the men

VIVA THE BRAZOS KID!

following us. He is not a cruel man, just a desperate one. For the same reason, he now holds you prisoner. I do not agree with him but I understand him.'

These words came from Bill's elbow in a soft, throaty Mexican-accented voice which contrasted greatly with the harsh tone with which Don Alonzo had addressed him. He swung round in surprise to see the newest arrival in the camp looking at him with earnest eyes. For a moment he found himself gazing into their brown depths, drowning in their dark beauty. But then his previous anger and frustration at his own helplessness caught up with him.

'And how would you know all this?' he asked jeeringly. 'Is he your man?'

'No, *señor*' she replied simply. 'I know this because Don Alonzo is my brother.'

Bill was still recovering from the surprise of this when Juan grabbed up the reins of his mount and swept him off with the others, leaving only the two bushwhackers clambering over the boulders as they sought out good vantage points from which to launch their deadly assault.

Sheriff Delaney scratched his stubbled chin dubiously as he viewed the pass ahead.

'This is a good place,' he announced to no one in particular, 'for an ambush.' The rest of the posse looked at each other in disbelief. Yet more delay from their overly cautious chief! The outlaws would be miles ahead at this rate and they would never

44

recover the town's hard-earned cash. The lawman sensed their discontent and made a snap decision – against his better judgement, it had to be said.

'OK,' he allowed. 'We go in. But stay well strung out and keep your eyes peeled. If there's some guns in there, it's as well we spot them before they spot us.'

With these words of admonition, the men made their way gingerly into the claustrophobic confines of the narrow ravine. The sheriff's words still rang in their ears, but once they got into the pass and saw the walls rise above them menacingly on either side, like giant jaws ready to suddenly close on them and swallow them up for ever, somehow the old codger's wariness did not seem so misplaced, and many wished they had listened more carefully to his forebodings. Not a sound could be heard as the shadow of the ravine enveloped them and they moved through its twisting course wordlessly, constantly craning their necks upward to search the rocks around them for any sign of hostile movement. Once there was a sudden rustling overhead and some of the men had their guns half-drawn before a raccoon poked his dark ringed face curiously over the lip of a high ledge.

'Sure thought for a moment that was a bandit with a mask on,' joked one of the men nervously.

'That crittur's lucky he didn't get hisself plugged!' laughed another.

Soon they were nearing the end of the ravine. Ahead of them they could see a spill of light where the ground opened up again. An unconscious sigh of relief went through the column of riders. The sight of daylight meant that the end of their passage through that place of darkness and potential danger was almost at an end. Then it happened.

A single shot rang out, made thunderous by the echoing walls of the ravine, and one of the posse fell heavily to the ground along with his horse. This was followed immediately by a fusillade of fire, the rapid cracks of the rifle mixing inextricably with the noise bouncing off the rock face, so that it sounded as though a hundred guns were being discharged at once and from several directions. Maddened by the din, horses reared up in panic, dumping their riders unceremoniously into the dust, then making a mad bolt for freedom from that place of death and mayhem. Several of the men still in the saddle struggled for control of their mounts as they tried to figure out where the shooting was coming from; this was not from any warlike wish to engage their hidden enemy but rather to determine in what direction it would be best to flee. As usual it was Sheriff Delaney who restored some order to the chaotic situation.

'Get off your broncs and get into shelter!' he yelled.

It seemed the best thing to do in their plight. His men needed no second bidding but hastily dismounted and flung themselves behind cover with guns drawn, their eyes anxiously seeking out the position of their ambushers. Left at sudden liberty, the rest of the horses rushed *en masse* from the scene and, as the clatter of their departing hoofs faded from the canyon, an unexpected hush fell over the place. Crouched behind a large boulder, Delaney carefully scanned the cliffs on either side. The gunfire had ceased as abruptly as it had begun and there was no sign of the attackers. Maybe they were playing a waiting game, trying to lull those trapped below into exposing themselves before a further murderous fusillade erupted. It was funny, though: as the lawman looked around him to check on his men, he could see that none of their number was dead or even injured. One of their animals had been killed and the rest driven off but apart from that they were none the worse for wear. Either the bushwhackers were very bad shots or. . . .

The grizzled lawman slowly stood up, provoking a barrage of warnings laced with expletives from his frightened colleagues.

'Get your fool head down, boss.' . . . 'Yuh tryin' to get yourself killed or somethin'?' . . . 'Dang ol' fool.' This last was said in a cautious whisper but deliberately loud enough to be heard by the target of the insult.

'You can come out now, boys,' said the lawman ruefully, 'If them *hombres* had meant to kill us, we'd all be buzzard meat by now. Fact is, they just meant to slow us down, maybe make us give up altogether. That's why they run off our horses. We'll lose half a day, maybe more, just roundin' them up again. Not to mention the fact we're now shy of one.' He nodded in the direction of the fallen pony. 'I guess we'd better get started right away, this is gonna take some time.'

Dusting himself off with his battered Stetson, the dogged oldster started off in the direction of their spooked ponies. The others in his band emerged from their hiding-places with considerably more caution. What the chief said made sense, but it was hard to shake off the feeling that unseen bandits still lurked in the crags above them, ready to send a volley of death into their shaken ranks. But when no storm of bullets met them, they rapidly scampered to catch up with their leader. This man appeared to know the enemy a lot better than they did and it was evidently safer to be with him than anywhere else.

As for Delaney, he forged ahead with a vigorous stride that belied his advancing years. But all the time his mind was occupied elsewhere. His imagination was beginning to shape a picture of the opposition: they were well-led and ruthless when needs be but not mindlessly bloodthirsty. This time they had spared their pursuers in the hope of discouraging them, but next time it could well be a different story. He had no intention of giving up the chase at this early stage, but they would have to be a mite more careful in future. No amount of money was worth the life of one man but these outlaws had already killed twice and they had to pay for that. How high that price would be and how far he would have to go to make sure they did, remained to be seen. But he sure enough intended to find out.

CHAPTER 6

A few days later Bill found out at last what Don Alonzo had in mind for him. The bandit approached him around mid-morning and handed him his gun belt with the pistol still in the holster. For a few wild seconds Bill actually dared to hope that, at last, he was being granted his freedom. But the next words he heard cruelly dashed that illusion.

'There is a town near here called Whiteford, my friend. In it there is a bank. Today, along with my *compañeros*, you are going to rob it.'

Bill started in astonishment, which quickly turned to indignation. Did this jumped-up Mexican outlaw think that he was ready to join him and his rag-tag bunch of miscreants on such short and, in the main, unpleasant acquaintance? His brow darkened and the grip on his newly restored weapon tightened involuntarily. Don Alonzo read the parade of changing emotions passing over his captive's face and he broke into a grin of amusement.

50

'Go ahead and draw,' he said, teasingly. 'Two seconds after, you would be stone dead. But if you are tired of life and would like a hero's death in a blaze of gunfire, be my guest. My men will readily oblige.'

Bill checked his anger and looked around him. The rest of the gang were watching him curiously to see what he would do. But he also noticed that their hands were poised close to their revolver butts. He would stand no chance if he were foolhardy enough to go try anything now. His shoulders slumped in defeat as he released his hold on his weapon.

Don Alonzo immediately seized the six-shooter and, with a flourish, flipped open the central cylinder to reveal six empty chambers.

'You don't think I'd be stupid enough to give you a fully loaded gun, do you?' he said with a mocking laugh. 'No, this is just a toy, a pretence to throw some dust in the eyes of the law and send them chasing off in the wrong direction after someone who does not exist – a phantom of my own making. I shall give him a name, something like. . . .' he furrowed his forehead in thought before his face cleared and he looked up. 'Yes, you come from near the Brazos River, do you not? Well then, we will call him the Brazos Kid. And you, my good friend Beel, will be that man!'

The raid on the bank at Whiteford went exactly according to Don Alonzo's carefully laid plan. Accompanied by three of the hidalgo's henchmen, including the ever-vigilant Juan, the quartet entered the building, where Bill, who was the only maskless one, had been instructed to brandish his empty pistol and announce a hold-up. After that, the others took over the rest of the robbery, moving with the practised precision of long experience. Only Juan held back from assisting the others, ostensibly guarding the door, but in reality his gun pointed unobtrusively in Bill's direction. As for the latter, he was forced to watch helplessly while his 'gang' cleaned out the collected savings of all the honest, hard-working folk of Whiteford. To the staff and customers of the bank, it looked as though he was overseeing the whole, nefarious enterprise but the truth was that he was as much a helpless pawn in the affair as they were. Even if he were so foolish as to try anything, there was a serious risk that innocent folk might get hurt and he didn't want to take the risk of that happening. So he was forced to stand by and let it all take place in his name, though the victims of the stick-up must have wondered how someone making so much easy money still managed to look so glum.

When the outlaws had secured all the booty, and were making their way out through the door, Juan stepped forward and, with a deliberate gesture, fired his gun into the ceiling of the room, showering everyone in a cloud of plaster and sending several ducking for cover. Pleased at the melodramatic effect this produced, he flashed his dazzling but somehow sinister grin.

'Congratulations,' he declared, 'You have just been robbed by the Brazos Kid.' Here he indicated the hapless Bill with an airy wave of his pistol. 'The roughest, toughest, most ornery desperado this side of Hell. Mind the name, *amigos*, the Brazos Kid. You'll be hearing a lot more of it.'

It was a florid and histrionic speech, delivered in the mechanical fashion of a bad actor mouthing unfamiliar lines as the Mexican struggled over the alien, gringo language of the script that Don Alonzo had carefully coached him to deliver. But it had the desired effect, as the cowed occupants of the bank looked on in terrified wonder at the subject of this extravagant boastfulness – an extremely mortified and irate Bill. When Juan was satisfied that everyone had had a good look at the so-called 'Brazos Kid', he fired another shot into the air and with wild whoops and more gratuitous shooting skyward, the gang fled town.

After that first raid, more followed and a pattern began to develop. It soon became obvious to Bill what was going on: Don Alonzo, as he made his way north from Mexico, had reconnoitred a series of suitable towns for these robberies. None was too big to have much law or, for that matter, a huge amount of cash in its bank vaults. In most cases there would be only one bank in the place anyway! But the band were steadily accumulating a substantial sum through these daring hold-ups and their reputation was growing. Or rather, the Brazos Kid's reputation was growing. For Don Alonzo always made sure that some sign or note from the Kid was left at the scene of each crime.

Soon posters with crude likenesses of the Kid began to appear, though these varied in quality and tended to exaggerate the ferocity of Bill's somewhat mild features. More worryingly, the reward payable on the Kid's death or capture started to rise, and with it, Bill's fear regarding his ultimate fate. What would happen when he had outlived his usefulness? Would the gang simply kill him and hand his body over to the authorities to collect the bounty on his head? If that were to happen, it would surely occur some-where towards the end of their journey, for it was clear that, slowly but surely they were now making their way back to the Mexico–USA border. Evidently Don Alonzo and his henchmen were intending to return to their homeland where they could live for quite a spell off their ill-gotten gains in considerable comfort and style.

It was also clear to Bill that the Brazos Kid scenario had not been part of the original plan. But it had chimed in well with Don Alonzo's intentions. Like this, the authorities would be looking for a white outlaw-chief rather than a Mexican. Even if Don Alonzo were unlucky enough to get caught, he could plead that he was just an underling of the real villain – that devil called the Brazos Kid – and probably escape with some lighter sentence. As regards the Kid himself, there could be no mercy for such a noto-rious scoundrel. Hanging would be the only suitable penalty for his heinous crimes.

But then something happened that threatened to wreck the whole elaborate scheme. The gang had just hit another small town called Earlston and were on their way out when all hell broke loose. The sheriff here was a little more wary of strangers than his counterparts in the previous burgs and, on seeing some not-so-respectable-looking gents entering the stockmen's bank, had hurried around town to rustle up a posse. Thus it was that a parcel of armed men were waiting on the miscreant band as they emerged into the daylight after their latest stick-up. Immediately a storm of fire erupted on the main street and, if it hadn't been for some nifty defensive shooting from the Mexicans and some conversely bad marksmanship from the nervous townspeople, there would have been a massacre on a scale not seen since the Dalton boys got ambushed at Coffeyville. As it was, one of the gang toppled over on to the sidewalk, killed outright by a shot through the heart, while another grasped his leg in pain and uttered an oath but managed to stay in the saddle as his panicked bronc bolted out of town.

As for Bill, there was nothing he could do to retaliate against the deadly stream of lead directed towards him. Even if his gun were loaded he would have been reluctant to fire back at honest citizens trying to protect their own property. Instead he made a run for his steed, jumped up on its back and, stooping low, dashed for the nearest way out from that deadly spot. He might have made it too, were it not for the fact that a stray shot winged his mount, which instantly fell to the ground, propelling him several feet into the air before he too crashed earthwards. He didn't notice much else about what happened next, except that for a short time he felt a sickening wave of agony shoot through his body before darkness spread over him as he settled into a welcome oblivion.

When he came to Bill found himself in an unfamiliar place, surrounded by four grey walls and a set of wrought-iron bars. It didn't take much savvy to figure out where he was and Bill uttered a groan as he sat up, both from the pain that this prompted in his battered body and the realization of his grim predicament.

That noise attracted the attention of his jailer, a tall, weather-beaten man with greying hair and moustache and a not unkindly expression on his face. He approached the bars and peered through them with a grin.

'How are you doin', Brazos?' he asked mischievously. It was all too plain from Bill's demeanour how he was feeling. The cowboy's heart sank even further when he heard that dreaded name. So they had already pegged him for the notorious, mystery outlaw!

'What the hell happened to me?' Bill asked, as he cautiously felt his aching head to check for any wounds.

The sheriff's grin widened.

"Don't worry none, you're in pretty good shape considerin'. Nuthin' but a few bumps and cuts and one hell of a headache from your fall, I'll wager. I had the doc look you over already. You'll soon be well enough to attend your own hanging.'

The lawman's grim humour at his expense failed to amuse the cowboy.

'I don't suppose it would do any good to tell you that I'm innocent,' he ventured, hopelessly.

'Nope,' replied the sheriff definitively, 'it wouldn't. Accordin' to all my prisoners I haven't arrested a guilty man yet.'

'What happens to me now?' was Bill's next worried query.

'Not too much for a while,' answered the sheriff cheerfully. 'I've informed the authorities and a judge is on his way to preside over a trial. That'll take a few days though. Meantime, you'll just sit tight here, relax and enjoy my wife's home cooking. May as well make the most of what's left of your life.'

On this hearty note the lawman retired to his office, leaving Bill to stew in his own melancholy thoughts. He never imagined that he would rue the day that he escaped from Don Alonzo's clutches, but the situation he found himself in now was even worse than his time with that Mexican brigand and his bunch of cut-throats. There at least there had been some hope of salvation, whereas here, in this grey, miserable cell, there was no hope of release except at the end of a length of hemp.

He was still mulling over his situation as darkness fell, as the cell became even gloomier without the comforting presence of what little daylight had penetrated to it. The only illumination now available was whatever lamplight managed to filter through from the sheriff's adjoining office. Soon even that disappeared as the lawman locked up his doors for the night and retired home, no doubt to sample the cooking of his spouse, which he had earlier commended to his prisoner. As for Bill, all he had seen so far in the way of sustenance was a few stale crusts of bread and a pitcher of water. Not that it mattered to him, for he had little appetite anyway in these present depressing circumstances. He was just going over in his mind for the umpteenth agonizing time how it was that he had come to this pretty pass when he heard a rustle at the cell window, then a familiar voice addressed him in a sibilant hiss.

'Hey, gringo!'

Bill jumped to his feet.

'Yeah?' he called out excitedly.

'Hssst!' came back the reply, in a tone of alarm. 'It is I, Juan!'

Bill had heard the Mexican speak English only rarely. Evidently he struggled with it now, as his voice sounded strained and hoarse. But harsh as the effect might be, it was pure music to the hard-pressed cowboy's ears, for it surely meant that Don Alonzo had sent his trusted lieutenant here to save him. But then another thought suddenly flashed into his mind: what if the Mexican was here to silence him? To make sure that he didn't reveal what he knew about that renegade hidalgo and his murderous henchmen?

He didn't have much time to consider the matter, for the next word that his saviour or perhaps assassin uttered was a crucial one.

'*Pato!*'

There was a scuffle of retreating footsteps as the deliverer of this cryptic message beat a hasty retreat, possibly disturbed by a patrolling deputy or merely an innocent passer-by. For a few brief seconds Bill pondered this curt message. *Pato . . . pato . . .* he'd heard the word before; it was Spanish for some kind of bird, something they'd eaten on the trail in fact. The meaning came to him just about the same time as he detected an ominous fizzing noise from just outside the prison wall. With a start, he realized that this was the Spanish for duck – which he proceeded to do with alacrity as a tremendous explosion rocked the jailhouse to its very foundations. It seemed the callous outlaw chief was prepared to risk Bill's life for the sake of a childish joke!

Luckily Bill had had the presence of mind to throw himself under the narrow cot that served as a bed in that otherwise bare room, or he himself would have taken the full force of the blast. Now he emerged, coughing and spluttering into a fog of dust and smoke, ears ringing and lungs bursting from the lack of oxygen, but not in any way seriously harmed. From the surrounding dimness, a figure suddenly appeared, grabbed him by the arm and propelled him over the rubble of what would have been the outer wall of the cell. Already, frightened and angry voices were being raised behind them as the towns-people rushed out of their homes to find the cause of this sudden disturbance. But the fugitives made it safely to a pair of waiting horses where Juan helped his still stunned companion up into the saddle before leaping on to his own mount and, leading the animal of the other man behind him, made off at a gallop into the night.

By the time the citizens of Earlston got to the scene of their wrecked jailhouse, all that could be detected of its former inmate was the sound of distant hoof beats fading into the distance. However, buoyed by the success of his mission, the Mexican could not resist one last act of bravado. As he fled he took the time to shout over his shoulder a wild yell of triumphant defiance:

'*Viva* the Brazos Kid!'

The townsfolk looked at each other in wonder-ment. Could anyone hold this elusive outlaw? Or, like some mythical will-o'-the wisp, would he always slip through the grasp of his captors to disappear yet again amidst darkness and confusion? Little did they know that there was headed their way at that very moment a man determined to make sure that this would definately not happen.

CHAPTER 7

Bill's welcome back at the camp was, to say the least, muted. Only Don Alonzo seemed happy to see him, the others acted as though he'd never been away.

'Ah, Beel,' exclaimed Don Alonzo on seeing him. 'How kind of you to rejoin us! We have been missing you very much, is this not so, *muchachos*?'

The rest of the band just looked at him with weary indifference, as though they didn't care if they never saw him again in their lives.

Alonzo himself assumed a look of pained disappointment at this lack of enthusiasm for the return of the prodigal son, as he put a fatherly arm around Bill's shoulders.

'You must forgive my men, *amigo*,' he said. 'They are – how do you say it? – a mite put-out, due to the fact that we lost one of our comrades during the shoot-out with the agents of law and order.

Unfortunately, he was also the man carrying the loot from the raid, so that we came away empty handed. So, you see, it is hard for them to raise a smile at your own deliverance from the gallows. But me, I am delighted.'

He turned to Juan and gave him a wink and a hearty slap on the back.

'My true and trusted follower, you have once again served me well. Now, go take your fill of food and drink, you have both deserved it.'

Leaving the two men to make their way to the campfire and salvage what remained of the food left over from the evening's repast, Don Alonzo ambled off with a pleased grin on his face. Things were back on track again after recent minor difficulties and now they would continue as before. The money lost on the last robbery would soon be made up for on the next one and the reward offered on the head of the Brazos Kid would rise further, so that a big dividend would be forthcoming when that villain was finally delivered into the hands of justice. And he, Don Alonzo, a fine, upstanding pillar of society, would be just the man to accomplish this laudable task and collect that reward. But all in due course, for he wasn't quite done with the Brazos Kid yet.

As Bill washed down cold stew with lukewarm coffee, Don Alonzo's sister strode into view. She wore a cream-coloured top and elegant riding-trousers that looked well on her slim figure. Brightly polished riding-boots with silver spurs completed her attractive attire. Her hair, which evidently she had just washed, hung free in long, lustrous tresses over shapely shoulders and caught the gleam of the firelight as she passed. Tired and hungry though he was, Bill stopped in mid-mouthful and gaped at this vision of loveliness like a kid staring at candy in a shop window. For that moment, it seemed that time had just stood still and all he could see was the breathtaking beauty of this woman before him. She caught his look of admiration, hesitated and, for a moment, looked almost as if she might smile back. But then she recollected herself and swept on past, as if she hadn't noticed his return at all. But that second of hesitation was enough to give Bill some slight hope that this fabulous creature was aware of his existence and there might even be the beginning of some sort of bond of sympathy between them. Not a friendship, but a kind of pity and understanding that a queen might feel for one of the more unfortunate subjects in her realm. But even that would be enough for the lonesome cowboy, given his present isolation and wretched plight. Any slight crumb of comfort seemed like a feast to him in a desert bereft of any human warmth or affection.

But, like a counterblast to his recently raised hopes, Isabella's self-appointed protector *El Bruto* came looming into view, as usual close behind her, and cast him an ugly look of deep-seated hatred. It was obvious that he resented this insolent gringo so much as looking at his adored mistress. Not that he feared she would respond to the captive's yearning looks; he knew her too well for that. But he sensed that something in her felt the beginnings of pity for the plight of someone who had been made a victim through no fault of his own. It was the same compassion that she had shown to him when every one else had rejected him for his misshapen deformity and which made her retain him as her willing servant when any other woman turned from him in disgust. He knew in his heart that she would never feel any emotion for him except pity but that was enough for him. Or had been up to this moment. But now, for the first time, he had a rival even for this most lowly claim on his mistresses affections. And there was awakening in his heart, slowly but surely, the most dreadful hate of this rival in misery and a hardening resolve to get rid of him sooner or later, by whatever means necessary, so he could once again bask alone in the comfort of his beloved's solicitude.

Early next day a group of dusty, determined and grim-looking horsemen appeared on the main street of Earlston. Leading them was a squat, ugly man with a battered Stetson jammed down on his bald head, his eyes constantly on the move, questing for some-one or something in that just-awakening town. Close behind him rode a stony-faced Indian on a palomino, followed by a ragbag collection of cowboys and other more respectable types. This odd bunch of disparate characters had 'posse' written all over it and, indeed, this was what it was, for Sheriff Delaney and his men were once again hot on the heels of their elusive quarry.

They found the local sheriff glumly sifting through the charred and still smoking remains of his jailhouse. He looked up at the sound of approaching riders and gave a brief nod of recognition.

'Howdy, Delaney,' he said curtly. For obvious reasons he wasn't feeling in a particularly sociable mood, even though he knew the other man fairly well.

'Hi, Jeffers,' replied his fellow lawman, tilting back his hat and standing up a little on his stirrups to better survey the scene of devastation in front of him. 'Had a bit of an accident?'

'Could say that,' Jeffers allowed. 'I had the Brazos Kid here as my guest for a short while, but I guess he didn't appreciate the accommodation.'

'Yeah, I can see that,' commented Delaney. 'When did he check out?'

'Must have been about eight last night,' came the reply. 'Didn't bother using the front door.'

Delaney nodded gravely. He had heard that the man he sought was in custody and he had travelled all night to get to Earlston so soon, but it looked as though he was already too late. Turning in the saddle, he cast an appraising eye over his troops; they were worn out, deadbeat. He'd been pushing them hard to try and catch up with their quarry; now the disappointment that their long pursuit was still not over showed plainly on their weary, vexed faces. Like all good leaders, the wily old law-dog was tuned in to the mood of his followers. There was a time to goad and a time to reward. Now was the time for the latter.

'Boys, you've been riding hard and you deserve a break. There's a bathhouse we passed on the way in; go down there and get washed up, get your duds cleaned, then meet me at the saloon. We'll have a beer together and figure out what to do next. If you're willing, we'll spend the day here and relax a spell before movin' on – your choice. Think about it while you soak in a hot tub.'

In reality the oldster had already opted to stop the day in town. Their animals were exhausted, as well as the men. But it was good psychology to let them think it was a democratic decision. Meantime he and Yellow Dog would borrow a few nags and scout the trail to determine which way the fugitives had gone. That way they would have a good head start when they did set off in pursuit again.

He turned back to his colleague.

'Any chance of borrowin' a few men for my posse?' he enquired hopefully.

'You can ask, but I'd say you won't get many,' replied Sheriff Jeffers candidly. 'It so happens that the one gang member we shot was carrying the loot. They didn't get a cent of the town's money. Far as most folk in this town are concerned, there's no reason to risk their hides chasing dangerous outlaws if they ain't stole nothing.'

'What about you? You're the law around here. They dynamited your jail. Ain't you gonna do anythin' about it?'

'As regards that,' answered Jeffers, scratching his chin, 'I guess I should be kinda glad in a way. I've been after the town council for a new hoosegow for quite a while now. The roof on this place leaked and it was damned draughty in winter. Now the whole thing will have to be torn down and rebuilt – with a bit of luck, should end up with far better premises.'

Sheriff Delaney regarded his fellow lawman with scorn. Sure, what he said might be true. But in his position he would look at it completely otherwise. If a prisoner escaped his custody and destroyed his jail into the bargain, he would be out for blood and wouldn't let up until he'd caught the malefactor. This other constable was of a different ilk; all he wanted was a quiet time until the day he collected his gold watch and pension. Delaney knew the type and didn't approve. As far as he was concerned, being an officer of the law was a calling, not just a job. You had to be thirsty for justice and unbending in your dedication to achieving it. This man was just a makeweight, going through the motions of the profession in a mechanical fashion, never going beyond what was strictly necessary. He, Sheriff Nehemiah Delaney, was the genuine article and he would prove it by running to ground the very villain that his incompetent colleague had so carelessly let slip through his fumbling fingers.

'Well, we're gonna need fresh horses and supplies,' he remarked tersely. 'Any chance of getting those here? I'm plumb out of cash but I'll give you an IOU to reclaim from the authorities on my side of the line.'

'Sure,' answered Jeffers. 'But I reckon the county here will foot the bill. Despite what you might think, we don't cotton to criminals robbing our bank and wrecking our jail. Take what you need and just leave me the bill. I'll make sure it gets paid.'

Delaney tipped his hat in recognition. His fellow law-officer still had some sense of honour, he was glad to see. But that still left the hard and dangerous job of running down the Brazos Kid and his gang of cut-throats to him and his men. Still, it was better not to look a gift horse in the mouth. He had a feeling that this pursuit he had embarked upon would be a long and arduous one and he would need every little bit of help he could get to track down his elusive quarry.

'I'm obliged,' he managed to force out between gritted teeth, before turning his pony round and heading down the main street. Tomorrow would be time enough to take up the heavy burden of duty once again. Right now, he could do with a stiff drink himself and later wander down to the bathhouse for a dip in the lukewarm and dirty water left after all the rest of the posse had enjoyed their ablutions. Being a sheriff certainly wasn't much fun but, secretly, he was enjoying the thrill of the chase and eagerly looking forward to resuming the hunt on the morrow.

CHAPTER 8

Time wore on and, just as with any group of human beings, the outlaw camp settled into a familiar set of routines, which began and ended each day. Bill was now, unwillingly, a part of this schedule and had to fall in with the habits of his hosts, whether he liked it or not. Still, he was not one to give in to any tyranny and did his best to maintain his own independence and self-respect in the midst of a dangerous and diffi-cult situation. Only by a series of small gestures could he maintain this facade of freedom but he persisted in these to persuade himself of his own dignity despite his impotent helplessness.

Thus, from long-standing custom and to keep up his morale, Bill insisted on shaving each day, a prac-tice eschewed by the rest of the band except for Don Alonzo himself, who was fastidiously dapper. However, the cowboy's own shaving gear had been lost or discarded when his captors had rifled through his belongings, and now he had to endure the rough ministrations of Juan, who used his well-sharpened Bowie knife to remove any facial hair from his charge. This was a painful procedure for the unfortunate Bill, since no shaving cream was applied and the only lubricant was supplied by Juan as he spat on the blade and slapped it noisily against the greasy seat of his pants to give it an extra edge. Despite this, the knife often slipped and left Bill with a chin permanently covered with sore and unsightly nicks.

After observing this excruciating exercise one day, Isabella summoned over Juan and spoke to him briefly before giving him a little money from her purse. The grizzled bandit looked a little bemused but knew better than to disobey his boss's sister and immediately got on his horse and took off at a gallop. Late that day he returned with a mysterious brown-paper bag. Bill discovered the contents of this bag the next day when Juan produced a shaving brush and a large tub of cream from its interior.

Instinctively the cowboy looked around for his benefactress and saw her standing not very far away, apparently tending her mare, but actually watching him with a sideways look from under her long lashes, the beginnings of a smile on her lips. Bill himself broke into a wide grin of gratitude and, for a moment, it looked as though the haughty *señorita* might deign to respond to this spontaneous gesture. But she caught herself in time and turned away to give her animal's mane her full attention. Anyone nearby might have noticed that her face had

71

reddened ever so slightly and that her combing of her horse's mane was perhaps a bit too vigorous. But since there was no one there to witness this and Isabella would never have admitted to such nonsense, that small but significant moment went unnoticed.

However Bill was not hurt by this seeming slight: he was only too happy with her gift to him and was touched by one of the few signs of compassion he had received in his present unhappy predicament. Thereafter, shaving was far less of an ordeal and, though the budget had not stretched to a razor, Juan's pig-sticker glided effortlessly through generously applied foam.

Another of Bill's peculiarities in the eyes of his captors was his insistence on regular bathing. Each time the band came across any sizeable river, the mad gringo would plunge into it to cleanse both his clothes and himself. For their own part, they might douse themselves from time to time in order to cool off in the summer heat and get rid of some trail dust, but what was the point of cleaning grimy duds when they only got dirty again in next to no time? Only Don Alonzo was as hygienic as their eccentric prisoner, but then the hidalgo's laundry was taken care off by his sister, who even used their precious store of soap to wash his garments. Besides, Don Alonzo was an aristocrat and used to such things. But Bill? He was just an ordinary man such as themselves and, in their eyes, such preening was a vanity and an unnecessary waste of energy.

During one such stop there occurred an incident that was to have a profound effect upon Bill and his relationship with the outlaw band, and in particular with the haughty *señorita* who had lately and so uncharacteristically shown him such unexpected kindness.

They had come to a particularly wide and fast-flowing river where Don Alonzo decided to strike camp on its banks for the evening. It was getting late and they would have to seek a shallower fording place in the morning. In the dying rays of the sun Bill waded out thigh-deep and began splashing water liberally over his body, rubbing trail dirt from his face and hair and generally enjoying the coolness of the stream after a hard, hot day in the saddle. He felt the strong current pull at his legs, seeking to dislodge him and sweep him away in its powerful embrace. For a moment he considered giving way to its urgent pressure. After all, he was a strong swimmer; if he could get round the next bend, he was sure he could easily make it to the shore again.

Cautiously he looked back towards the camp. As usual there was Juan, rolling himself a cigarette whilst keeping a wary eye on him, a Winchester cradled in his arms. The Mexican had a fear of water and would never venture out more than knee-deep but he was as good with a firearm as he was with a knife and Bill knew that he would never make more than a few yards before his guard would be drawing bead on him and letting fly a deadly hail of fire. Besides, even if he did make it, where could he go without any food or weapon? The country around them was growing ever wilder and was full of unseen dangers. An agonizing death through hunger and exposure seemed the most likely outcome of any such foolish venture.

Still, in his desperation, Bill seriously gave consideration to the idea. This might be his last good chance of escape; once they got deeper into the badlands the chances of his getting out alive became ever more remote, whether he stayed with his kidnappers or made a bid for freedom. If he suddenly dived into the swirling torrent towards the middle of the river he might be able to stay submerged long enough to get out of rifle range. Of course there was always the chance that they would come after him along the bank, but it was thickly wooded in places; the pursuit would have to be on foot for no horse could penetrate those thickets. But then again, the water seemed to be increasing in force as it rounded the bend and disappeared from sight in a gushing frenzy of white foam. Who knew what lay around that twist in its headlong spate: rapids full of razor-sharp rocks? A towering waterfall? Certainly the deafening roar emanating from the coursing flood as it squeezed its way between the narrow chasm that lay a bit further downstream did not seem to bode well for anyone foolish enough to brave its perilous passage.

He was still deliberating on his best course of action, half-looking back at the shore to see if Juan's vigilance might slacken a little to present him with a chance to make a successful escape effort, when he thought he heard something above the din of the rushing waters – something that sounded like a faint cry. He turned round in time to see a shape flash by him, borne quickly past by the swirling current. The madly threshing limbs and pale hue of naked flesh suggested it was no inanimate thing or dumb animal that was in difficulty but a fellow human being. Bill did not hesitate to plunge into the surging waters in the wake of the rapidly disappearing figure. Whereas before it had been only his own life at stake, this time it was someone else's and this gave him the courage to do what he had previously balked at.

The next few moments were a blur of struggle and fierce determination as he felt the river's powerful grip upon him like a giant child who had suddenly found a new toy and was eagerly playing with it before casting it aside, broken and unwanted. Somehow he managed to keep a sort of control over his direction as he hurtled along round the river bend and, to his relief, he realized that here the river widened out again and the chaos and clamour that had characterized its progress through the narrow ravine had subsided into a decidedly gentler murmur as it went more sedately on its way. He looked around anxiously and immediately glimpsed the object of his quest some yards ahead of him. To his alarm, the

75

form appeared to be no longer moving but was floating face down in the water, seemingly without the
slightest sign of life. Bill felt a sickening spasm of
alarm. Had he risked his life to rescue a corpse? With
a few swift strokes he came alongside the recumbent
body and with a start he realized that it was a woman,
her long, black, matted hair floating on the surface
like a strange sea beast. He flung one arm around
her neck to raise her face out of the water and with
his other he struck out for the shore. Once there, he
waded out, dragging his burden behind him before
collapsing in the warm sunshine, thoroughly
exhausted by the physical and mental demands of
the last few crowded moments. As he crouched on all
fours, still recovering his senses, he heard a faint
moan from the figure stretched out beside him. So
she was still alive!

Two things struck him with almost equal force at
that moment. One was that this damsel in distress
was none other than the beauteous Isabella: that was
no surprise really, since she must be the only woman
around for miles in this remote and rugged country.
The other was that she was totally naked! She must
have gone for a swim upriver and got carried away by
the unexpected force of the current. Dumbfounded
by this turn of events and concerned as he was for
her safety, Bill could not help noticing the exquisite
loveliness of the creature stretched out before him.
He'd seen many a *risqué* painting of nude ladies
above many a saloon bar but none that could

compare with this – the real thing. It was with a real wrench that he managed to drag his eyes off her voluptuous form and got down to the pressing matter of ensuring that she stayed alive to enjoy her loveliness!

Bill had never received any instruction in how to revive a half-drowned human being but common sense told him to flip his patient over with her head tilted sidewise and then push for all he was worth on her lungs so that she expelled any water that might still be in them. Rough and ready as this remedy was, it seemed to work, for after a few moments of this treatment the woman came around a little and began coughing to clear her throat. In another few moments, her limpid eyes fluttered open and she made to get up, though she hadn't yet the strength to do so. At the same time Bill heard the sound of approaching voices and thought it wise to take off the jacket he was still wearing (he'd had no time to discard it for his impromptu dip) and drape it over the prone figure before him. Decency as well as self-preservation dictated this, for Don Alonzo might be a little put out to discover his sister naked with another man!

When the others in the gang arrived, Don Alonzo at their head, they discovered the gringo still standing over the figure of the half-dressed Isabella. They looked speculatively at the face of their leader; he was notoriously sensitive to any of his subordinates so much as looking at his sibling the wrong way and usually meted out harsh punishment to those he reckoned guilty of such an offence. How would he react to the seemingly compromising scene now before him? But the hidalgo was nothing if not a fair man – by his own lights. He looked hard from the still dripping wet cowboy to his half-conscious sister and immediately comprehended the import of the scene. Without uttering a word he advanced on her saviour and wrapped him in a warm embrace.

'Señor Beel,' he said, his voice thick with emotion, 'You have saved my beloved sister. How can I ever repay you?'

Bill was so taken aback by this show of feeling from the normally callous and flippant hidalgo that he looked closely at the hard-bitten bandit to see if this was just another instance of his cruel humour. But nothing except honesty and sincerity shone in the other's deep brown eyes and for a moment he was tempted to request there and then the small favour of granting him his freedom and the return of his hard-earned cash. But something within warned him against this course of action; it would be better if this offer came from Don Alonzo himself: in that way the promise would be more likely to be kept than forgotten once the warm glow of gratitude had worn off.

'*De nada*,' he replied, in one of the few Spanish phrases he had managed to pick up. 'It was nothing. I was only too glad to be of service to a man such as yourself.'

It was Don Alonzo's turn to be taken by surprise

and he scanned the face of his captive attentively. This was a reply such as he might expect from one his class of noblemen in his homeland, asking no favours but merely dismissing the greatest of services with a deprecatory shrug and a gracious compliment to the beneficiary.

Perhaps there was more to this simple cowpoke than he had imagined. From now on he would pay him more heed, for such nobility of soul was rare anywhere, but it was at a premium in the rude and uncultivated company he was nowadays forced to keep in his newly chosen profession of brigand.

At that moment Isabella came more fully to herself and looked in wide-eyed alarm at the circle of concerned faces around her.

'What . . . what happened?' she asked.

'You were bathing, *mi hermana*,' anwered her brother gently, 'when you must have slipped and got pulled in by the river. If it weren't for Señor Beel here. . . .'

Isabella regarded Bill with strange, wondering eyes.

'It was you who saved me?'

Unwittingly she had slipped into using the familiar form *tú*, used mostly with friends and family members. The other members of the gang noticed and exchanged significant glances. The other instances of using this term were with menials such as themselves but it was evident that from the new light of admiration and respect in the *señorita*'s comely eyes that she did not intend it this way with the *nortamericano.*

Before the young cowpoke could frame a reply, *El Bruto* came running up, red and sweating, his features contorted with fearful anxiety. Slower than all the others because of his awkward bulk, it was only now that he had managed to catch up with his comrades. In his blind panic he roughly forced his way through the group and relaxed only when he saw his cherished mistress, standing there, safe and well, before him.

'Ah, *señorita*,' he cried, 'I was so worried when I saw you fall into the river. I ran immediately to tell the others. Thank God you are alive!'

Instead of being grateful for this fervent proclamation of his relief, Isabella turned upon her unfortunate well-wisher with a look of thunder.

'You were watching me bathe?' she hissed through clenched teeth, her fists balled in white-knuckled fury. 'How dare you? I told you to guard my clothes, keep your distance and warn anyone else off too. Instead you were spying on me yourself, you pig!'

Realizing his mistake, the unhappy man tried to defend myself.

'No . . . no, *señorita,* I . . . I thought I heard a cry. I ran to the bank and you were gone. I assumed you had been swept away by the water. I was so afraid we had lost you. Now I am so glad to see that you are safe.'

'Yes, thanks to this gentleman' countered Isabella,

turning to Bill with an altogether softer look in her eyes and wrapping his coat more warmly round her.

Suddenly aware that his sister was still only half-clothed in front of his gaping men, Don Alonzo barked out an order. One of the men took off his poncho and handed it to the girl. She slipped this over her head and deftly removed Bill's now sodden jacket, returning it with a grateful smile to its bashful owner. The voluminous poncho served to cover up a substantially greater part of her shapely anatomy, much to the secret disappointment of the majority of the men there. Then they made their way back to the camp where Don Alonzo sent *El Bruto* off to recover his mistress's missing garments.

The misshapen Mexican went on his way, quietly seething at his recent humiliation. Yes, it was true that he often spied upon Isabella as she bathed, instead of keeping watch as instructed. But what man of flesh and blood wouldn't? She was ravishingly lovely – he felt deep within him a consuming desire for her that nothing would ever destroy. He knew that his cause was hopeless; besides his repulsive ugliness he was of low birth, born in a mud hut while she had been born in a mansion. But this very distance, this unobtainablity served only to quicken his yearning for her with a desperate, despairing love.

In the past he had comforted himself with the reflection that, although he could not have her, she was so haughty and so proud that it seemed unlikely that she would ever deem any man good enough to

win her favour. But now this interloper, this gringo
had arrived and suddenly things were different. He
noticed that her gaze would linger on the handsome
stranger when she thought no one was watching.
Except that, as far as she was concerned, *El Bruto* was
always watching and he saw what was going on all too
plainly. Her present of the shaving gear to their prisoner he was prepared to ascribe to her innate,
though often well-hidden, kindness to those less
fortunate than herself. But the way she had looked at
Bill just now when that lucky devil had had the good
fortune to be in just the right place at the right time!
He, *El Bruto*, would have given his life's blood for
such a look. But instead, he had been rewarded for
his rescue alert with her withering contempt and
scorn: she had branded him a sneaky Peeping Tom.

As his thoughts turned towards his new and more
successful rival, *El Bruto* felt hatred grow in his
tortured heart. Besides being younger and better
looking than he was, this man had saved the life of
his beloved and made him look like a fool in front of
the others. He felt himself burn with rage and jealousy as he imagined him dragging her from the river,
his hands all over her sacred person, no doubt gloat-
ing and drooling over her defenceless nakedness as
he, *El Bruto*, in anguished desperation, got up a
rescue party, only to arrive too late to get any credit
for his efforts. Pretty soon he had convinced himself
that the gringo had not saved the girl but had
assaulted her in some underhand way without any

one but himself noticing it. But *El Bruto* would not let him get away with it. The newcomer might have pulled the wool over every one else's eyes, even the proud Isabella's, but *he* would not be deceived. He would wait and watch and, when the moment was right, he would pay back this insolent upstart in good measure. And when he was done with the gringo the cowboy would be in no condition to please another woman again. That much he would make sure of. And that tantalizing thought brought a smile of pleasure to the loathsome villain's lips for the first time in many days.

CHAPTER 9

Sheriff Delaney's posse was not a happy one. They had been wandering in a wilderness for days now without catching any trace of the fugitives they sought. Even Yellow Dog seemed to be stumped by the elusiveness of their prey. Some of the more rebellious of the group began to grumble aloud at the parlousness of their position. They were getting further and further from home, with little to show for their pains except weary limbs and diminishing supplies of both coffee and patience. Unsurprisingly, those who had been most vocal in calling for a speedy pursuit in the aftermath of Hal Jenkins's untimely demise were now at the forefront of the faint-hearts who wanted to call the whole thing off and return home. They suddenly remembered that they'd never much liked Hal, or that brother of his who had got killed in the stick-up. Wasn't he the town drunk, who never had a dime to his name and was always harrying respectable citizens such as themselves for the price of a drink? Such are the vagaries of the human memory, that we choose to remember those things which suit us according to our present wants and needs. The men were tired now and discouraged; this Brazos Kid was like some kind of illusion who vanished just as you thought you had him in your grasp. They doubted if they'd ever get him; likely he was long gone, maybe even dead, and they were merely wasting their time in chasing a phantom.

Experienced in human nature as he was, Sheriff Delaney was not blind to what was going on. The surliness of the men in getting up in the morning for another hard day's riding, the silences at mealtimes instead of the usual joshing and banter, the ill-humoured grumbling at trifling mishaps were all warning signs. He knew that there was trouble coming but kept his own counsel. It would be better to let the thing boil up of its own accord, in his view. That way he could clearly identify with the chief trou-blemakers when the time came and, if necessary, get rid of them.

As for himself, despite being twice the age of most of the rest of the men in the posse, the lawman was enjoying himself in his own grim way. He was a man of action and chasing bad men came naturally to him. This was a lot more challenging than his usual humdrum duties as sheriff in a small township and he relished the excitement of the hunt and even the hardships he had to endure along the way in order to track down the object of his quest. Being on the trail was no burden to him – in fact, it reminded him of happier, youthful days when he had pursued errant Indians under General Phil Sheridan. Those heady days were now long gone but the memory of the camaraderie and common purpose that had pervaded those campaigns still lived with him and came back to him now like a ghostly echo.

But the men he was with now were no disciplined, tough band of soldiers; they were ordinary townsfolk who were used to soft feather beds and linen sheets, not hard earth and a saddle for a pillow. By bluff and guile he had got them this far, but even he could see that they were near the end of their tether. The only question was where and when they would finally crack. But, wily and experienced leader of men that he was, he still had a few aces up his sleeve. He cannily kept these to himself but, when the moment arrived, he would play them with all the skill and bravado that he had and, he hoped, trump all the arguments of the would-be mutineers.

The old lawdog did not have too long to wait. Early one morning, as they were getting ready to break camp, the men seemed more sluggish than ever and after exchanging glances, a few of the more outspoken malcontents approached him.

'Sheriff, the boys would like a word with you,' said one, a tall, sallow store-owner called Travers.

'Oh, yeah,' replied the lawman, feigning inno-cence as he continued tightening the cinch on his riding rig. 'What about?'

Travers exchanged another look with his partner, a red-headed saloonkeeper called O'Flaherty.

But the Irishman stayed silent, so Travers reluctantly continued with his spiel on his own.

'The fact is we've been chasing this Brazos Kid character for quite a while now and we ain't caught sight nor sound of him in weeks. He could be long gone and we're just runnin' after shadows. Some of us have businesses, most have families; we can't afford to be wastin' time out here lookin' for a ghost. We discussed the matter after you turned in last night and decided it's time to turn back. We ain't doin' no good out here.'

Sheriff Delaney eyed the man in a deadpan fashion.

'And what about the money that was robbed from the bank? It belongs to you and the rest of the citizens of our town. Maybe for some it was all they had. Are you so rich you can afford just to write it off?'

'As regards that,' countered Travers, an air of triumph in his voice, 'everybody knows that bank money is insured. Some big company back East will pick up the tab and pay us all back. For them, it's just loose change; they won't hardly notice the difference.'

Delaney appeared to hesitate at this and, for a moment, the rebels thought they had won the argument. But the shrewd oldster was merely acting out a part already rehearsed in his mind – that of the reluctant bearer of bad tidings.

'I hate to tell you boys this,' he said, scratching his chin in apparent perplexity, 'But I had a word with Matt Wilson, the bank manager, before we lit out of town. He was a real worried man. Seems he neglected to renew the bank's insurance policy and we're not gonna get a red cent back on the money that got stole. He made me swear not to tell anyone unless I absolutely had to, but in the circumstances. . . .'

The two spokesmen for the disgruntled posse exchanged a look of consternation then simultaneously returned their gaze to the sheriff, the same thought playing on both their minds. Was the sly old fox playing some kind of game on them? Spinning them a tall tale to get some extra effort from his exhausted and demoralized followers? They certainly didn't put it past him, for Delaney could be ruthless in his pursuit of what he considered justice, even to the extent of bending the truth a little to get what he wanted.

But the lawman's face was a mask of passivity and they found no help there in determining the veracity of the shocking assertion he had just made to them.

Like a cunning general seizing upon the sudden confusion of his enemy, Delaney chose this moment to deliver another piece of news that he hoped would swing the battle of wills entirely in his direction.

'One other thing I think you should know,' he said, pulling a crumpled piece of paper from his hip pocket and smoothing it out carefully. 'I picked up this here wanted poster for the Brazos Kid in the last town we passed through. You can see for yourself – the reward for his capture, dead or alive, now stands at five thousand dollars. A few men have dropped out so there's ten of us now; that comes out at five hundred dollars apiece. I ain't lookin' for no extra share just on account of bein' in charge.'

Travers and O'Flaherty looked closely at the poster. Sure enough, in bold letters was printed that fabulous amount of cash on offer for the apprehension of the Kid. Even the more prosperous of the posse scarcely made that amount in a year. And if, heaven forbid, a few of their number were unlucky enough to get killed during the taking of their outlaw quarry, then there would be even more left to share out among the survivors. They still didn't know whether to believe Delaney's story about his supposed conversation with the banker, but there before them, in black and white, was plenty of reason to continue with their quest – 5,000 reasons in fact!

Delaney watched the different emotions pass across the face of his opponents and an almost imperceptible smile creased the corner of his lips. He could see the fish were hooked and now was the time to reel them in.

'Well, boys, now you know all the relevant facts, what do you think? Do we go home empty-handed and let the townsfolk know that most of them are ruined? Or do we go back like heroes, with the bad guys in tow, the bank money and five hundred dollars each?'

Put that way, there could only be one answer. The two erstwhile malcontents grinned sheepishly and the Irishman spoke for the first time.

'Well now, Sheriff, sure we wouldn't like to let you and the rest of the community down. We had our moment of doubt there for a wee while but I think you've convinced us of our civic duty. Wouldn't you say, Travers?'

The other man nodded vigorously.

'We'll just be gettin' back to the other lads and put the case to them but I'm sure they'll all see the good sense of what you've said.'

Delaney watched them go through narrowed eyes. His mixture of bluff and promise had worked – for the moment. It was likely that trouble might rise again but at least now he knew the main source of the unrest: it was that pesky, rebellious Irishman behind it all. He had let the more gullible Travers do all the talking but it was obvious that he was just the puppet of the real master of the mutiny who had just stood silently beside him, while all the time monitoring what was being said. However when the real moment of decision had come, O'Flaherty had tipped his hand by stepping in with a clinching decision, to which Travers could merely mutter his meek assent. Now he knew how the land lay, the sheriff would keep a close eye on this snake in the grass, keep him away as much as possible from the others and, if it came to a fire-fight, Delaney knew which of his men he was prepared to send first in to harm's way. . . . Not that he would ever risk any man's life unnecessarily, but if it came down to it, he wouldn't lose any sleep over the demise of one more trouble-maker: the way he saw it, there would still be more than enough of them left in the world if O'Flaherty was gone.

One other factor that the sheriff omitted to mention in his reasoning with his unhappy under-lings but which weighed greatly upon him, was the lately discovered presence of a female in the outlaw band. It had crossed his mind to appeal to the more chivalrous nature of these supposed pillars of the community – if it was the case – that this woman had indeed been kidnapped and was being held against her will. But the world-weary cynic in him told that it would be a waste of breath to broach that particular subject; when it came right down to it, most people put their own interests first and principles second. Sure, it might make them feel good to picture them-selves as some sort of Sir Galahad off to the rescue of a damsel in distress. But the sad fact was that saving innocent maidens usually brought no pecuniary reward and would involve some considerable personal risk to their own hides. For the likes of Travers and O'Flaherty, these would always be the chief considerations.

But for Delaney, the plight of this unknown lady did bring fresh complexities to an already dangerous

91

situation. If and when they ever did catch up with the fugitives, how could he guarantee her safety in the inevitable fireworks that would erupt? He would just have to play it cautious until he was clear about her exact status within the gang. If she were one of them, she would have to take her chances along with the rest. But if she were an innocent victim, he would do his best to save her from the guns of both his own men and their foes. Perhaps, if they could locate the enemy camp, he and Yellow Dog could sneak in Indian-style and snatch her away under cover of darkness. Decidedly dangerous but, in the circumstances, well worth the risk. Or perhaps they could do a trade-off with the bad guys: the life of the girl and the money in return for their liberty. But he could not see someone as ruthless as the Brazos Kid going tamely for that one – the desperado would likely fight to the death before accepting such a deal.

As the permutations and possibilities of what might happen swirled around his brain, the lawman gave his head a sudden shake as if chasing away these thoughts like troublesome flies. As usual, he knew that when the time came he would instinctively know the best course of action to follow. Why give himself a headache for no reason now? But he was sure, at the back of his mind, that sooner or later he would have to make some life-or-death decisions, and who lived and who died would very much depend on him!

CHAPTER 10

Things changed a great deal for Bill after the incident on the river. He was accorded a great deal more freedom, rarely tied up during the day and was treated much more like an honorary member of the gang than a prisoner. The attitude of Don Alonzo was a lot friendlier, or as friendly as a man of his aloof character got with anyone outside his own class, and the others went along with that, accepting him almost as an equal. But Bill wasn't fooled by this apparent camaraderie. For a start, they were now in a remote, savage part of the territory; a man would be a fool to try and make it out of here on his own, unaided and without provisions. He could wander for days in its untamed vastness and end up dying an agonizing death, his body being eaten by wild animals. Bill suspected that the bandits knew that and were counting on it to keep their unwilling guest in their clutches.

Moreover, the unwinking gaze of Juan was still

constantly upon him; whatever the feelings of the inscrutable Mexican were towards him, Bill still had no doubt that the faithful henchman would kill him in an instant at a mere nod from his master. It was an uncomfortable notion that his life hung on the whim of another man, but one that he just had to live with until he stood a reasonable chance of escaping this uneasy situation.

But there was another reason for Bill's reluctance to take his chances and flee, one that he was unwilling to admit, even to himself. A sort of understanding began to grow up between the proud sister of his captor and this humble cowboy being held against his will. Increasingly she took to riding alongside him on the trail, occasionally remarking on the natural beauty of the countryside around them. From his long years in the saddle and also from his own natural curiosity, Bill knew a fair bit about plants and wildlife and was able to answer a few of her childlike questions about the wonders they encountered. Luckily her English was somewhat better than his Spanish – her education being rather more rounded than his rudimentary schooling – so they were able to communicate fairly easily.

To his astonishment, Bill found himself rather coming to like this seemingly cold and petulant *señorita*. He began to understand that her air of superiority and separateness from other folk was only her way of protecting herself from unwanted attention in the rough, all-male company in which she found herself. Beneath it all, he suspected that she was rather lonely, not just for the company of others of her sex, but indeed for anyone who would lend a sympathetic ear to her often childish but harmless prattling on the everyday events of the journey, or share her infectious enthusiasm for the unusual sights and sounds they daily experienced in this unspoilt part of the country. After his own long isolation, Bill was only too glad to have her company, despite the possible danger it put him in with the madly jealous *El Bruto*, who constantly threw him murderous glances. She was easy on the eye, good company and kept his mind off the dire trouble he was in. For the moment at least, he was content to allow himself the teasing and merriment of incipient romance, which so contrasted with his recent despair and darkness of mood.

Don Alonzo looked upon this growing relationship with a tolerant eye. He was pleased to see his sister happy and laughing again, even if only for a short time. Before, she had been getting moody and withdrawn, unused as she was to the hardships of the trail and the constant all-male company of others so different from herself. Now that she had a more congenial companion, this would perhaps absorb her energy and emotional needs, always difficult to satisfy in a highly strung woman. And there was the added bonus that this might prevent the gringo captive from contemplating flight as his attention was diverted by the attention of a beautiful female.

The canny Mexican had little worry that the flirtation would develop into anything more serious; he knew his sibling too well for that. She would often be attracted by someone new and different in her life and for a while would permit herself to be carried away by the feelings of the moment. But deep down inside, she knew that she was a noblewoman, the scion of ancient, aristocratic Spanish blood. When she eventually married, it would be to one of her class, of impeccable lineage and, preferably, substantial wealth. This adventure with a humble cowpuncher was merely a passing fancy, a young girl's whim before settling on a more realistic and appropriate choice for a long-term mate.

This had better be the case anyway, Don Alonzo grimly told himself, for sooner or later the *norteamericano* would have to go. When the reward became sufficiently great, he would be handed over to the law, either dead or alive. At first there had been no doubt in his mind about which this would be; the man knew too much concerning their gang and its methods, it would be impossible for them to continue to operate this side of the border if he were to remain alive. But now things had changed: Bill had saved Isabella's life and seemed to be gaining rapidly in her affections. He himself was not immune to the simple, straightforward character of his captive, although he would not let this cloud his judgement if it was a matter of his own survival. No – when it came right down to it, there was no real option: their prisoner would have to die. Quickly and mercifully if possible, but die he must. The only problem would be trying to explain this necessity to his sister. Perhaps the man could be shot 'while trying to escape' or perhaps the insanely jealous *El Bruto* would do the job for them by slitting the throat of his hated rival. Either way the gringo had to perish – the only question was when and how. Little did he suspect that the danger to Bill's life was more imminent than he thought. However, it would come not from him or any of his unsavoury band but from others, very close now, and even more callous and bloodthirsty in their lust for death and destruction.

As Bill's intimacy with Isabella grew, so too did the animosity shown to him by her self-appointed bodyguard, the loathsome *El Bruto*. Although the men had not exchanged more than two words, Bill could see shining in his eyes a deadly hostility and naked urge to do him mortal harm. It did little to increase his sense of well-being and safety but there was little he could do about it. Even if he wanted to, he could hardly prevent Isabella from chatting to him or bringing him a coffee or smiling at him, for that was all their interaction consisted of so far. And he was not prepared to hurt a woman he was beginning to care for by brutally telling her to leave him alone. That would be both cowardly and unkind and Bill was neither. Besides, though he hardly admitted it to himself, he'd come to depend upon her cheerful presence to lighten the darkness of his difficult and lonely circumstances – alone in the presence of hostile strangers and in constant fear for his life. And her luminous beauty and feminine glamour had become like a drug to him that he could scarcely do without.

Ironically, the previously irksome and unsettling vigilance of Juan now served as a reassurance and a comfort. As long as the stony-faced Mexican kept his basilisk gaze upon his captive, Bill felt safe and protected, for he knew that, cold-blooded killer as he was, Juan was also fanatically loyal to his leader. Provided Don Alonzo desired it, the gringo cowpuncher under his charge would live. And since, for reasons of his own, the brigand-chief did desire it, Bill was for the moment secure.

Bill could not help feeling, however, that there was something more to *El Bruto*'s bitterness towards him than mere jealousy. He seemed to harbour an unreasoning hatred towards not just him but all gringos for some reason, and to despise anything or anyone from north of the Rio Grande. Why this was, he couldn't fathom but he felt that, no matter what he did, the misshapen Mexican would continue to want him dead, so he might just as well do what he pleased.

Lately Isabella had taken to giving Bill lessons in Spanish, a language that the cowboy was keen to learn, both to alleviate his boredom and also because it could be of vital use to him in trying to ensure his own survival. The rannie was an enthusiastic pupil, though not a particularly able one, and his frequent blunders and mispronounciatons were a constant source of amusement to his teacher. Hence the sound of her laughter ringing out was not an unfamiliar one as she chuckled at his latest misuse of her native tongue. Bill did not mind her merriment at his errors; it was good to see her full, red lips curved in a good-humoured smile, pearly teeth exposed – even if it was at his expense. Sometimes he even exaggerated his gaucheness of expression, just to win a silvery peal of her laughter. But always on such occasions, when he looked beyond the cheery glow of the campfire light, he could just about make out a pair of baleful eyes staring intently at him, like a cougar eyeing up prey before making its deadly leap. He couldn't make out the face but knew instinctively who it was and each time he inadvertently gave a shiver of disquiet at this unsettling sight. At last he could bear it no longer and broached the subject with Isabella.

'What's eatin' that feller, the one you call *El Bruto?* He looks at me like he wants to tear me apart and throw the pieces to the four winds,' he asked her one evening as they sat around the fire.

Isabella glanced out into the darkness where, as usual, the subject of Bill's query was lurking, his gaze fixed intently upon them. Then she looked back directly at the man facing her.

'He is jealous,' she said simply. 'You saved my life, which was his job, and made him look bad because of that. Now he would like to kill you.'

Bill's breath was taken away by the uncompromising bluntness of her reply.

'Well, thanks for that information, though it wasn't something I didn't already know,' he responded, with an air of irony that escaped his more serious companion. 'But it isn't just that, is it? He's mighty fond of you, if you don't mind my saying so. I don't think he likes seeing us together so much lately.'

Isabella looked at him for a moment or two and a hardness entered her face that he had not seen there for a while.

'He is like most men – I showed him a little kindness, a little pity and soon he ends up thinking he owns me. I belong to nobody, I am my own woman and make my own decisions who I spend time with – not him.'

Bill was taken aback by this outburst of haughty pique.

'I hope you don't think I'm like that,' he said apologetically, aware that he also was an object of her compassion.

Isabella knotted her forehead as if thinking about it for the first time.

'No,' she said after a while, 'you are different. You do not seek to make any claim on me but one of friendship. It is for this reason that I like you.'

So saying, she put her hand upon his and, for the first time, the pair physically touched. Bill was surprised by the jolt of excitement that this most innocent of gestures caused him. Until now he hadn't realized what a hunger there was in him for contact with a sympathetic fellow human. And the fact that this other person was an attractive female made the thrill that ran through him all the more potent.

Perhaps Isabella felt something of the same emotion, for she quickly withdrew her hand again and, for a while, the two looked away from each other and into the dwindling heap of burning twigs that was their fire. New thoughts and sensations were springing up in each of them and now they needed a moment or two of calm to sort these out.

Then Isabella abruptly arose and announced, a little coldly it seemed to Bill, that she was retiring for the night. She left the confused drover pondering his newly aroused sentiments. Was he starting to fall in love with this girl bandit (for she was after all part of the gang holding him against his will)? And how did she feel about him? Not particularly warmly at the moment, judging from the peremptory way she had taken her leave. But perhaps that was merely her own attempt at denial of a passion that was undoubtedly beginning to grow between them.

The permutations of this complication to an already fraught situation were just causing the simple cowpoke to develop a first-class headache. So, tilting his hat over his face, he pulled a blanket up to his chin and settled down for the night.

There would be plenty of time to figure things out in the morning; now he needed his rest and strength, for who knew what fresh challenges tomorrow might bring?

From his resting-place nearby, *El Bruto* had observed all that passed. For several nights in a row now he had sneaked away from the main campfire to spy upon his mistress and her new-found friend, the accursed *norteamericano*. Lying in the cold and darkness, with only a poncho and a bottle of whiskey to keep him warm, he had been silently observing the pair. What he'd seen did not please him. When Isabella put her hand upon that of the gringo it was as though she had laid it on his heart and was squeezing the life from it. Unconsciously, his own hand stole to a large, sweeping scar which ran down his cheek from temple to jaw; it was burning now, as if it were freshly made, and his mind went back to how he came to acquire it, a long time ago, from compatriots of the one now trying to take his beloved Isabella from him. . . .

He had been travelling on his own north of the border, making his way home, when darkness had fallen. To his relief, he spotted a distant campfire; it was dangerous to sleep alone on the prairie at night. He'd joined the owners of the fire, three white cowboys, who'd welcomed him according to the laws of hospitality that universally prevailed in this wildest of places. The men told him that they were *vaqueros*

102

rounding up mavericks that had strayed from a nearby herd. But the Mexican noticed a running-iron protruding from a saddle-bag and wondered at their story, for this implement was the classic instrument of rustlers. He believed them all right, when they claimed they'd been gathering up cattle, but whether the cows they been seeking were their own or someone else's, there he had his doubts. Nonetheless, it was none of his business. He was no saint himself and certainly wasn't about to interfere in the illegal activities of others, especially if, with a little chicanery, he could share in their ill-gotten gains.

After a friendly cup of coffee and some chow, they settled to playing cards over a bottle of liquor and soon the visitor had amassed a large pot of his hosts' money. The atmosphere turned sour then – the cowboys were quite drunk and accused him of cheating. Of course, he had been but, in his own mind, that was beside the point. An argument developed and, before he realised what had happened, two of the men had suddenly pinned his arms behind his back and lashed his hands securely with some strips of rawhide.

Then their leader, a fat, coarse-featured individual, had put the running iron into the fire to heat it up. When it got white-hot he took it from the flames and spat on it. The spit evaporated immediately with a sinister hiss. The cowboy cast an evil eye on his helpless victim.

'Hold him real tight, boys,' he ordered grimly, 'I'm gonna mark this greaser for the cheat he is. That way, everybody'll know what kind of lowlife they're dealin' with.'

With a harsh laugh he advanced with the branding-iron in his hand. The Mexican struggled frantically but the leather only bit more deeply into his wrists, while the restraining grip of his captors dug hard into his arms. The glowing light of the metal came closer until it seemed to fill the whole world. He felt its searing touch upon his cheek and smelled the rancid stench of his own burning flesh, then merciful oblivion delivered him from the agony of his fiery torture.

When he woke up the next morning, the others had long gone, along with all his possessions, including his horse. They'd even taken his boots and most of his clothes. Still half-mad with pain from his burn, he'd wandered in a parched stupor for days before stumbling across the Rio Grande. It was there that Don Alonzo's band had come upon him, crawling south, almost naked and delirious. Isabella had taken it upon herself to look after the unfortunate wretch and had spent many days and nights nursing him back to health. For that, she had earned his undying love. But, by the same token, any man he perceived coming between them would earn his eternal hatred. It mattered not that he knew his case was hopeless; that she would never feel anything for him but a mixture of contempt leavened with pity. It was enough that he could be near her, see her, protect her. Anyone who threatened to take that privilege away from him would pay dearly. And if that man were of the damnable Yankee breed that had once caused him so much suffering, then his fate was indeed sealed, and he would not die an easy death but a long and cruel one. *El Bruto* would make sure of that!

CHAPTER 11

Bill was not the only one to feel himself to be under the glare of hostile eyes. As they penetrated deeper and deeper into the badlands, so did Don Alonzo's nervousness seem to grow. Every now and again he would halt, stand up on his stirrups and scan the surrounding countryside, which was thickly wooded and interspersed with rocky hills – ideal territory for an ambush. There was no definite reason for this caution, just an uncanny feeling, like an ache at the back of his neck, that they were being watched and that the onlookers did not mean them well. The men could not but help noticing his edginess, so he addressed them during a rest stop.

'Listen, *muchachos*, there could be dangerous animals around. It would be wise to be vigilant. We may be safe from the law here but in a wild place like this, there may also be many hungry creatures that do not mind at all the taste of a man's flesh and blood.'

The way he phrased this warning might have been ambivalent but Bill was left in no doubt that the 'dangerous animals' the outlaw chief referred to could just as easily be human as beasts. Either way, peril appeared to be stalking their tracks and it seemed just a matter of time before it finally struck.

Even as Don Alonzo issued this dire warning to his followers, atop a nearby high pile of boulders girdled by some pine, four pairs of eyes were fixed steadfastly upon him and his followers. Their gaze was cold, savage and calculating but they belonged not to wolves or lions or bears but to that most cruel and predatory of all species – man.

By and by the eldest of the foursome ceased his intense vigil to stretch, scratch himself and turn his head sideways to project a liquid stream of tobacco with unerring accuracy on to a lizard innocuously sunning itself on a nearby rock. He grinned with satisfaction as it scuttled away in alarm.

He must have been in his late sixties, though it was hard to say how much of this impression was due to the rough, turbulent life he had led, as opposed to the natural effects of ageing. His hair was long, grey and greasy and he bore the unkempt, bushy beard of a mountain man. The buckskin suit he wore was stained and grimy and fitted him so tightly that it was hard to imagine he ever removed it, almost as though it had become a second, stinking skin to him. However, the Bowie knife that hung from the belt

107

around his waist seemed, in stark contrast to the general slovenliness of his appearance, gleamingly clean and well looked after, as did the Sharps rifle slung across his broad shoulders. This man was obviously a hunter – one who made his living by killing other animals for their meat and skin. But there was also an air about him that he might not stop there and would be prepared to bloody his hands on different game – providing the reward was tempting enough.

'A bunch of greasers, a woman and a white man,' he said to no one in particular. 'That's a mighty strange party. Wonder what the hell they're doin' way out here?'

'Maybe they're dodgin' the law like us, Pa,' suggested one of the others, a small, swarthy man with a ferret-like look about him.

'Or just plain lost,' sniggered the youngest of the four, a tall, skinny youth with straw-coloured hair, an idiot grin and vacuous eyes.

'Who the devil cares,' broke in the last member of the group. 'They got good guns, horses and most likely money – not to mention the woman. . . .'

Unlike his brothers, for this unholy bunch were actually all family, this man was of strapping build. But his powerful physique was not matched by any corresponding strength of character and his features were coarse, ugly and unintelligent, not improved any at that particular moment by the look of greed and lust that burned there.

The old man stroked his ample beard thought-fully.

'Jeb's got a good point there, a helluva good point. These is lean times for us, boys, mighty lean times. If the good Lord provides some tasty plums for the pickin', who are we to turn down his infinite bounty?'

He cast his eyes heavenwards in nauseous piety. But then the fulsome look of thankfulness vanished from his ill-favoured countenance to be replaced by a more habitual expression of malevolent craftiness.

'But it ain't gonna be easy, mind. We need to be careful. Them varmints is well-armed; they look like they're expecting some kind of trouble. For the moment we just follow them, see? We just watch and wait and, sooner or later, we'll get our chance. Then we strike and strike hard. No man left alive, but try to save the woman if you can, don't need to tell you why. Just do what I say when the time comes and every-thing will turn out real sweet. You hear me, boys?'

The others nodded enthusiastically. The booty was not to be scorned but mainly they were thinking of the woman. It had been a long time since they'd enjoyed that particular pleasure . . . and it was rare that they had the money to visit a bordello on their few visits to the nearest town. Now here was a beauti-ful female practically landed on their lap – it was too good an opportunity to miss. And they wouldn't mess up the chance. When the time came they would kill every man without hesitation and then this poor, unsuspecting girl would be at their tender mercy.

And, given the nature of these scoundrels, that mercy would likely be in very short supply indeed.

That evening Bill had a very peculiar dream. He imagined himself stuck in the centre of a great spider web, its grey strands stretching off in every direction until lost from sight. His limbs were inextricably stuck in this loathsome trap and, no matter how much he struggled to release himself, he seemed just to become more entangled in the thick, viscous fibre that held him ever more securely. Then, horror of horrors, he felt the structure vibrate around him as if at the approach of something climbing over it towards him. Too terrified to look, he sensed that this had to be the monstrous maker of this accursed web, come to claim the prize of its diabolical cunning. Closer and closer it got until he felt its vile presence hovering right over him, maw open to consume its helpless victim. One hairy tentacle fastened itself upon his shoulder to steady him for the deadly bite and he instinctively shuddered beneath its powerful grip. He opened his mouth to scream but something blocked it, choking him, and with a start he suddenly came awake.

Instead of the beady, evil eyes of the giant spider that he was fully expecting to behold, Bill found himself instead looking into the infinitely more attractive gaze of Isabella, who had one hand upon his shoulder and one across his mouth to smother his incipient cry.

'Sssht!' she ordered imperiously. 'The others should be sound asleep by now but we must be as quiet as possible.'

So saying, she produced a small dagger from the top of her boot and quickly but efficiently cut though the bonds on Bill's hands and feet. Then, putting her finger to her shapely lips as an admonition to keep up the silence, she took his hand and led him quietly through the sleeping camp. A quick glance around on Bill's part reassured him that the entire gang was indeed slumbering peacefully, though he couldn't help but notice, even in this hour of extremity, without the usual accompaniment of loud snoring. They made their way stealthily into the darkness until they reached a small copse of trees. There were two horses tied to one of these, both laden with enough provisions to last several days. Bill turned to Isabella questioningly.

She returned his look with a disarming smile.

'I slipped something into the coffee of the men earlier. When they wake tomorrow, they will have splitting headaches, but otherwise no other bad effects. By then we will be long gone and they will never find us.'

Bill remembered now that Isabella had made the coffee that evening and insisted on serving each man personally, including those on guard. He had put this down to mere kindness and solicitude for her companions but now he saw her real motive. The next question was obvious and must have showed in

111

his face for she answered him before he could frame it.

'Why? Because you saved my life, because you got mixed up in a bad situation through no fault of your own and because . . . I like you.'

This last was said with a degree of hesitancy, as if it were a difficult thing for her to admit and, in the darkness, he couldn't be sure that her face didn't redden a little as she said it. As if to cover her embarrassment and also to forestall his next question, she hurried on with her explanation.

'And I will be accompanying you because I'm not sure how my brother will react to this betrayal. I do not seriously think he would harm me, but it would harm his standing with his men if he let me go unpunished. I am saving him that necessity by going with you. Don't worry though, at the first opportunity we can go our separate ways and I will cease to be a burden to you.'

Bill opened his mouth to say something, then wisely shut it again without uttering a word. Isabella had obviously thought this all through and made up her mind. He could remind her of the potential dangers of the trail ahead and beg her to stay and throw herself upon the mercy of Don Alonzo. But he knew that this would do no good. Isabella was not the kind of woman to change her mind once she had set it to a course of action. Besides, if they made it to safety there was the chance that Isabella might consent to stay with him and, maybe, if things went well, agree one day to be his wife. His money was back in the camp, concealed in one of the saddle-bags but Bill was content to leave it there. Let Don Alonzo keep it as a sort of compensation for the loss of his beloved sister; for his part, Bill hoped that he might have found a greater fortune yet than any he had lost and one that might still make the whole crazy, frustrating experience of the last several months all worth while.

They mounted the horses and slipped stealthily from the camp. Once a little clear, they had a hurried, urgent discussion on which direction to take. Due to the inhospitable nature of the terrain, it was impossible to travel to the north or south; both were cut off by precipitous mountains. So the choice was either to go west – back they way they had come – or to proceed onward east, which was the direction they had been following. In the end they opted to go west. This had two advantages: first it was a track they knew since they had already passed that way, ahead lay totally unknown territory; and second it was less likely that Don Alonzo and his men would backtrack to pursue them, since it ran contrary to what were obviously carefully laid plans and it would also expose them to the danger of running into Sheriff Delaney's faction. Of course, there was also the danger that Bill and Isabella might cross trails with that doughty lawman but there were only two of them and, with a little bit of wariness, they stood a good chance of getting through unobserved while the posse chased their larger quarry. In the euphoria of their escape and the warm glow of each other's company, they had forgotten Don Alonzo's words concerning the hidden dangers of this savage land, where wild beasts roamed and death was never far away. Now, as they made their joyous way to freedom, they did not imagine that the greatest peril to them would not come from either Delaney or Don Alonzo, but from men of more vicious breed altogether, who even now were close upon their heels.

CHAPTER 12

Bill and Isabella travelled through the rest of the night and kept going even after dawn. They figured it was best that they put as much distance as possible between themselves and their erstwhile companions. It wasn't until darkness was again falling that they let up on their relentless pace and picked a spot to camp for the night. Both were dead beat and their horses were in not much better condition. Once they had dismounted, Isabella started to forage for some kindling to build a fire and brew some hot coffee, but Bill stopped her.

'Best not,' he said ruefully. 'A fire would only attract attention and that's what we need to avoid at the moment. Your brother might be out there; that posse is, for sure, and God knows who else.'

He instantly regretted saying this last, for immediately a look of alarm entered Isabella's comely features. She did not so much fear either of the groups Bill had mentioned. With her womanly wiles, she was sure she could handle those men as she had so many others. But the thought that there might another unknown danger lurking in the shadows that were starting to thicken; that idea frightened her more than anything.

'Don't worry none,' he said reassuringly. 'I'll be standing guard tonight. Not even a gopher will get near without me blasting his head off.'

This was said in the hope of raising a smile to her ruby lips and he was not disappointed. It was however quickly followed by a frown.

'I don't want you to stay awake the whole time. You will wake me after a few hours and I will take my turn, yes?'

Bill was about to turn down this offer but then thought better of it. It was no good trying to play the hero in these circumstances when both their lives were at stake. Truth was, he was dog-tired and knew he could never keep awake all night, no matter how he tried. They were in this situation together and would both have to share the hardships equally if they were going to survive.

'All right,' he agreed, 'I'll take the first watch. I'll give you a call in about four hours.'

Without further ado Isabella turned in and almost instantly dropped off to sleep. Bill wrapped himself in an old blanket and hunkered down atop a nearby boulder. Gradually the first faint stars began to appear in the clear firmament overhead. As he watched them Bill shuddered and wrapped the blanket around him more tightly. It was going to be a cold night, he thought glumly, and without so much as a hot drink to chase off the chills or the friendly glow of a campfire to keep him company. But now, at last, he was free and surely that was worth a little discomfort. Not to mention the beautiful woman now in his charge, asleep nearby in the darkness. It was his responsibility now to get her to safety. After that . . . who could tell? Maybe she would come visit him at his ranch; it wasn't big but had fine grazing and lots of water. The house where he lived wasn't fancy, it was true, but he had always planned on rebuilding it some day when he got himself a wife and started to raise his own family. With a bit of luck, that time might not be far off. These pleasant thoughts and dreams so beguiled him that he ceased to notice his physical discomfort and started to drift off into that trancelike state between waking and slumber. A few times he caught himself out and suddenly sat upright again, shaking his head as if to shed the weariness that was engulfing him. But Nature, as always, had the last say and eventually the exhausted cowboy's body succumbed to forces greater than his own and his head slumped forward in the unmistakable sign of complete surrender to sleep.

Soon after, sinister figures began to stir in the depths of the night and to creep cautiously toward the sleeping duo. One of these worked his insidious way up behind Bill's immobile figure and approached his unwary victim from behind. Stooped though the man was, it was impossible not to notice his gigantic size, made all the more obvious when, reaching the object of his stalking, he suddenly reared up to his full height and dealt the defenceless cowboy a vicious blow with a cudgel he was carrying in his huge fist. Simultaneously three of his ruffianly comrades sprang upon Isabella, one seizing each arm while the third thrust a rough gag into her protesting mouth. Despite fighting like a tigress, she was quickly bound up and slung unceremoniously across her own horse. All this was accomplished silently and efficiently within the space of a few seconds. These men were obviously adept in the ancient and disreputable art of kidnap.

Only then did the eldest of the group, who had led the attack on Isabella, walk over to Bill's prone figure to examine it dispassionately.

'He dead?' he asked in a casual tone.

Bill's outsize assailant grinned evilly.

'Probably. I sure fetched him a good one.'

As if in answer to their callous speculations, Bill uttered a pained groan as his head lolled to one side. His hair was matted with copious blood and his face was pale and drawn but there was no doubt that the hardy drover was still very much alive.

Jeb looked at his father questioningly.

'Will I finish him off, Pa?' he asked eagerly, his fist already tightening over the grip of his club. It was obvious that nothing would give the sadistic giant more pleasure than to ruthlessly put down a helpless

118

and wounded man.

'Naw,' replied the older man. 'He might be useful to us. I want to find out who these *hombres* are and what they're doing here. Then you can do what you like with him.'

The older man was not less cruel than his monstrous offspring but a little more canny. It was true that they could probably extract all the information they needed from the woman but it would likely require some unpleasant methods and he wanted to spare her as much of that as possible. He had in mind for her an altogether different purpose and for that it would be better if she could be preserved in good physical condition.

Jeb looked a bit disappointed that his immediate bloodlust was not to be sated but knew better than to challenge his pa's authority. Besides, the old man had as much as promised him first go when the time came for their victim to be dispatched. He would enjoy that when the time arrived; it would give him something to look forward to. For such was his perverted and twisted mentality that he derived pleasure from such acts of brutality, especially when he had the opportunity to practise his sick fantasies on a fellow human being.

It didn't take them long to reach the tumbledown shack that served as home and headquarters for this outcast clan. Tucked away in the backwoods, it was difficult to reach from the main trail and, unless one knew it was actually there, it would be hard to find unless by sheer luck. But that was the way these rogues preferred it, for they had good reason not to be found and liked the feeling of security their isolation gave them.

The place certainly wasn't much to look at: a ramshackle rectangle of log walls topped by a sod roof. But it was spacious enough and, with its small windows and sturdy oak door, had been built to withstand a minor siege if necessary. Anyone planning to take the house by storm would have his work cut out, which was exactly what its creators had intended.

The front yard was lined with frames of hazel rods upon which were stretched the skins of various animals to dress and cure them, their carcasses hung from the porch to season them in preparation for eating, while the bones of past kills were strewn in abandoned heaps around the edges. All in all, the impression was one of an open-air slaughterhouse, with the attendant stench and aura of death.

Inured as they were to their grisly surroundings, the Calhouns seemed delighted to get back to their noisome hovel and gave a whoop of delight to be back home. But Isabella couldn't help giving a shudder of horror when she laid eyes on this ill-omened abode before she was hustled into its dark interior as if being immured in a living tomb. As regards Bill, he was barely conscious when he was dragged from his horse and manhandled into the building. Only when he was fully roused again would he realize the full terror of the situation into which Fate had once again thrust him. For him, it seemed, that old adage was perennially true – out of the flying-pan and into the fire.

When Bill eventually did come round completely, with the aid of a cup of cold water flung across his face, he found himself in the heart of this forbidding lair. It was sparsely furnished with a few pieces of crude furniture, including the chair to which he was securely lashed. In front of him stood the imposing figure of the head of the Calhoun clan, his heavy brows knitted in a fierce frown, for all the world like an eagle about to swoop on a defenceless sparrow. Between him and Bill was a battered wooden table upon which sat a wicked-looking bullwhip and a massive, well-thumbed Bible. It was an incongruous pairing but one which summed up the twisted psychology of their owner.

Calhoun wasted no time with niceties.

'You see this, mister?' he said, holding up the thick coil of leather so that Bill had a better view of it. 'It'll cut through a man's skin like a knife through butter. Ain't nothin' you won't tell me after a few licks of this. So save yourself a lot of pain and answer all my questions. I ain't an unreasonable man. Tell the truth and maybe I'll let you live.'

Bill didn't believe the old reprobate for an instant. He realized that the moment he ceased to be of use to this bunch of miscreants, they would get rid of him in very short order. At the moment only their leader's curiosity lay between him death. Desperately he played for time as his reeling brain sought some way out of this dire predicament he was in.

'Sure, sure, I'll tell you everything,' he promised. 'But first tell me what happened to my fiancée?'

He lied about their relationship in the faint hope of giving her some protection.

The old man looked puzzled at this unfamiliar term. Then enlightenment broke.

'Oh yeah, you mean that fancy piece we caught you running away with. Don't worry none about her. We got her stashed somewhere safe. Won't nothin' happen to her if you co-operate.'

'Is she hurt?' Bill persisted, both out of genuine concern and to play for a little more time.

'Naw,' answered the other, 'She's right as rain. Started squawking away in Spanish when we took off her gag. Can't get no sense from her. Don't she speak American?'

Bill shook his head emphatically, divining that this was a ploy on the part of Isabella to give her some slight advantage over her captors. The girl was playing it smart. Now Bill could tell his interrogator anything without fear of being unwittingly contradicted by his female companion if they questioned her separately. With the security of this knowledge, he could concoct a story that might keep them alive until rescue or escape. Bill wasn't a skilled liar but common sense told him that his best chance would come from mixing up the truth with some sort of fiction that would give this bloodthirsty band some kind of incentive to keep them alive as long as possible.

'OK,' he said, 'I'll talk. Ask me anything you want.'

'Good,' countered the mountain man, laying down the whip on the table. 'I like a man who don't waste my time. First off, what's a white boy like you doing way out here in the badlands with a bunch of greasers?'

'Have you ever heard of an outlaw called the Brazos Kid?'

'Nope,' came the frank answer. 'Me and my boys don't get no newspapers out here and, even if we did, none of us read too good. And the last time we were in any kind of town was last Fourth of July celebrations, near a year ago.'

'Well, I am the Brazos Kid,' asserted Bill, surprised at how easily that particular lie came to him. It was almost as if several weeks of playing the part, albeit unwillingly, had imparted some sense of that false identity to him.

Though he observed that this particular bombshell had absolutely no effect on his listener, he continued with growing confidence. In those few seconds of prevarication, he'd hit on a scenario that might just appeal to the weak spot of this gang of scoundrels – their greed – and guarantee him and Isabella a stay of execution for at least a few days.

'Things were getting a little hot for me and my gang down in Mexico, so we decided to come north for a spell. We pulled a string of bank robberies in small towns west of here – not much in each but it's all added up. But the law was getting too close for comfort here too – in fact there's a posse on our tails right now.'

Bill paused again to see if this piece of information caused any alarm in the man facing him. He was pretty sure that this old rogue would be none too keen on any encounters with officers of the peace. But Calhoun kept a poker face, he was too wily a hand to show his feelings so readily.

'Anyway,' Bill continued, 'things came a bit unstuck in a place called Earlston. The townsfolk got wise to us and a god-almighty firefight blew up. One of my men got wounded, another killed and we all took off in different directions. As luck would have it, I ended up with the money, our biggest haul yet, but with a bunch of riled-up citizens on my tail. I managed to give them the slip for a bit and rejoin the rest of the gang at a spot we'd fixed beforehand. I told them that I'd lost the loot during the chase but I'm not sure they believed me. But with a posse breathin' down our neck, there was no time to discuss the matter. We lit out for the wilds and that's how we wound up here.'

'Very interesting,' sneered Calhoun, 'but I ain't heard anythin' yet that's gonna save your sorry hide.'

Already he was reaching across for the evil-looking weapon he had set on the table earlier.

'Wait!' said Bill, feigning a panic that, in the

present circumstances, it was not too hard to fake. 'There's more.'

Calhoun continued to pick up the whip and flexed its coils in his powerful hands. He was enjoying the power of terrorizing what he perceived as a helpless victim.

'Go on,' he ordered, 'but it had better be good. My patience is bein' sorely tried.'

'The thing is,' said Bill, lowering his voice and leaning forward confidentially, 'I never lost the money. I hid it in case I got caught. It's still there now. That's why I snuck out the way I did. Wasn't anybody gonna share that bonanza except me and my sweetheart.'

His eyes gleaming with avarice, the trapper also leaned forward.

'So where's it hid?'

Bill let out a snort of derision.

'You think I'm some kind of a fool to let out that kind of information for nothin'? Why, my skin would be hangin' up outside with the rest of them critters and you'd be on your way to collect that booty for yourself.'

Calhoun lunged forward, his face livid with thwarted anger. Now he was showing his true nature, despite his previous calmness, and it was not a pretty sight.

'You're gonna tell me, mister. Or I'll take the whip to you right now and tear the flesh off your every bone!'

The younger man seemed unmoved by this violent threat.

'Won't do you no good. I hid it real well. Even if you got a description of the location out of me, it would be useless. You'd still need me there to show you the exact spot where it's buried.'

Calhoun stopped and scanned his captive's face for any sign of deception. But the open, honest face of the cowpoke in front of him displayed not the least trace of deceit. For a few moments Calhoun's anger struggled with his greed, but the latter was the stronger of the two and he eventually regained his composure.

'What proof do you have of any of this, mister? You don't look like no desperado to me. And that yarn you just told me sounds like it came straight from a dime novel.'

At this, Bill produced his trump card.

'Look in the wallet inside my saddle-bag,' he said triumphantly, 'you'll find all the proof you need there.'

The old man eyed him suspicious but duly fetched the bag and fished out the oilskin pouch tied up with string. When he unfurled it, a few sheets and a clutch of newspaper clippings fell out on to the table. Calhoun paid no attention to the newspaper items – he couldn't read them anyhow – but picked up one of the sheets, which were of all-too-familiar appearance to him. It certainly wasn't the first poster of a wanted man he had ever seen; indeed he'd been the subject of a few himself in his time. The yellowing paper bore the image of a man along with the sum offered for his apprehension. Screwing up his eyes, Calhoun looked from this picture to its supposed subject, then back. Sure enough, the crude drawing bore an unmistakable resemblance to the *hombre* across from him, though depicted in a more villainous cast. It was hard to believe in fact that the clean-cut young man was actually the hardened criminal of the poster. But then who would have suspected that scrawny William Bonney, better known as Billy the Kid, or the mild-looking looking Jesse James would be among the most cold-blooded killers of their generation? Calhoun was finally convinced.

'OK, Brazos,' he conceded, with a new tone of respect in his voice. 'I believe you. Now what about getting that money?'

CHAPTER 13

It was a good thing that Bill had thought to save proof of his infamy as the Brazos Kid in the way of newspaper reports and the wanted posters. At the back of his mind he had the vague notion that they might be useful to him if the day ever came that he had to defend himself against the charge of being that notorious outlaw. He figured it would be an advantage to have a record of the misdemeanours he was being accused of if he was ever going to have any hope of rebutting the charges. But now, earlier than he had expected, these descriptions of his 'exploits' had come in unexpectedly handy. Without them the hardened criminal opposite him would not be regarding him with something verging on respect, ready to cut some sort of dealt his life in exchange for hard cash.

Taking stock of the situation he decided to use his leverage to the maximum.

'Before we go anywhere or do anything, let's

parley some terms,' he said firmly. 'First off, you gotta let me and my woman go free when we've got the loot. Second, the money's to be divided even – each man gets an equal share. That's fair, isn't it?'

Calhoun nodded vigorously, a little too vigorously. It was obvious to Bill that he would agree to practically any conditions since he had no intention of keeping his word in any case. But as Bill was of the same mind anyway, it didn't really matter. All that mattered was to gain a little time, no matter how little, to give him and Isabella a fighting chance of survival.

'We ain't lawyers and you say you don't read so good, so there's no point in puttin' any of this down in writin',' continued Bill smoothly, 'but if, as I expect, you're a God-fearin' Christian and if you're prepared to swear all this on the Holy Bible, I'll take your word on it and take you to the hiding-place.'

With alacrity, Calhoun took up the volume of the Good Book and, with loathsome sincerity, swore to Bill's demands. They both knew that the oath was meaningless – once the money was recovered, Bill was as good as dead. And as for the woman . . . death would be an easier option than what was in store for her at the hands of these blackguards.

Bill made one further proviso, which gave the lecherous old goat pause for consideration before he reluctantly granted his assent.

'One other thing is that I don't want you or your other boys layin' so much as finger on my girl. If that happens, the whole deal's off.'

Calhoun nodded somewhat hesitantly. In theory that didn't matter either, since the female would be at their mercy anyhow when they got what they wanted. Trouble was, his sons were not very good at waiting, especially if there was a beautiful woman at stake. Even his hitherto undisputed authority over them might not be enough. He would have to think of some stratagem to cool their ardour; but already a crafty scheme was hatching in his devious brain. He rapidly explained it to Bill in order that he could, through the medium of Spanish, explain the ruse to Isabella. For her compliance would be necessary if the plan were to succeed. Thus the two men who started out in mortal enmity wound up as uneasy partners; but it was a cynical alliance on both sides and each was aware that it could only end one way – in bloodshed.

Meanwhile the rest of the Calhoun clan were in disgruntled mood. No sooner had they made their triumphant return to their cabin with the two captives in tow, than Pa had ordered them out again to check the traps they had set earlier in the week. Once out of earshot, Jeb voiced the dark suspicion that the old rascal had just invented this pretext to get rid of them so he could enjoy the woman on his own. But none of them had the courage to defy their elder's authority and so they dutifully trooped off to do his bidding. They were right in surmising that

Calhoun wanted to get them out of the way for his own nefarious reasons, though not the particular one they had in mind. He had merely wanted to hear Bill's story first so that he could use the information to his best advantage; like all ruthless leaders, he knew that knowledge is power, and how it was presented to his followers was important in controlling their reactions.

When the brothers got back, their mood was, if anything, even sourer. The pickings from the trip were particularly poor, with only an undersized badger and two mangy possums to show for their pains. By way of consolation, they had bagged a few jackrabbits along the way for that evening's pot but, all in all, it was a poor return on their efforts.

To their surprise, they found their father genial and hearty, waiting to welcome them home. Even their pitiful tally of animals from the traps didn't seem to dent his jollity. Again the suspicion began to grow that the old rogue was in such fine spirits through having had himself a good time with their comely captive. But after his initial, overly effusive greeting, his next words surprised them and dispelled this illusion.

'Boys, I got an announcement to make. I've been thinking about it and I reckon the time's right to grow this family some. I got me three fine sons but now I want some fine grandchildren too. But I don't want no bastards – it's all to be lawful and proper in the sight of God and any offspring are to come from the state of holy matrimony.'

He stopped to see if his kin had grasped his message. Observing only blank faces, he explained in more basic terms.

'Meanin' that one of youse is gonna get hitched!'

Comprehension began to dawn on their bemused countenances.

'Now, in his bountiful providence,' the sanctimonious scoundrel continued, 'the Good Lord has delivered a bride to us. Now all we have to decide is which of you three gents is going to be the groom.'

The would-be suitors exchanged looks of wonderment. Marry the woman? Sure, they'd all counted on using her, or rather abusing her, for their own low purposes but to wed her? But the way Pa put it made sense. How else could a man create a family in this benighted wilderness? However, there were three of them and only one potential mate; who would be the lucky one? They returned their gaze expectantly to their patriarch. As usual, he would be the one to solve the problem.

Calhoun was pleased to see that they were falling in with his scheme and he proceeded with his lecture.

'The way I see it, boys, it's only fair that the lady picks for herself. Now you ain't exactly been properly introduced to her yet, so I want you to go get yourselves dickered up some and come back to the yard here in, say, an hour or so. I'll do the talking for you but I want you to look your best and be ready to show her your most favourable side for her to start choosin' who she wants for a husband.'

Only rat-faced Sal, the most intelligent of the trio, thought to raise the obvious objection.

'But what if she don't want any of us, Pa?'

His father gave him a withering look.

'Why, she'd be a fool to turn down any of you fine specimens of manhood. Besides, she knows what'll happen to her if she don't go along with it!'

With these menacing words, he turned on his heel and stalked indoors. It seemed to him his ploy had worked. As long as each son believed he was eventually going to get his hands on the woman, he would be prepared to wait and even defend any attempt on the honour of his 'intended' by the other two. With that much out of the way, he could rely on Bill's help in obtaining the hidden hoard of cash. After that, all the sham would be done and they'd do with the woman what they always did with everything that came into their possession – share and share alike.

At the duly appointed hour the Calhoun reunited in front of the house. Their pa held an impromptu inspection and quick conference with the would-be bridegrooms before Isabella was led out like a lamb to the slaughter. Standing on the veranda with Pa Calhoun, she had a good view of the aspirants to her hand standing in a row below her. The brothers had made some kind of effort to spruce themselves up, though with generally woeful results. Aaron, the youngest of the trio, had even dug out a suit from his teenage years. Unfortunately for him, he'd shot up a lot since then so that the sleeves and legs of his outfit were far too short, leaving his arms and legs protruding in a ridiculous manner and giving him the air of an overgrown schoolboy.

Sal, the middle son, had a mite more sense. He'd selected the cleanest duds from his limited wardrobe and even slicked down his hair with some cheap eau-de-Cologne he had put by for special occasions. But even his best clothes were still pretty shabby and he only ended up resembling a down-on-his-luck hawker – all that was missing was a seedy carpetbag.

As regards Jeb, the biggest, laziest and most arrogant of them all, he'd done little beyond combing back his lank hair and changing his shirt for a slightly less dirty one. A botched attempt at trimming the thick stubble on his chin had resulted in numerous nicks and grazes so that he had ended up looking, if anything, worse than before.

When Isabella surveyed this motley group of suitors, her first reaction was to laugh. But, wisely, she managed to restrain this impulse. The Calhouns might not take that in good part and Bill had primed her to play along with this farcical charade. So she pretended to treat this courting ritual with all due solemnity and looked impassively down on the upturned, hopeful faces turned to her.

Pa Calhoun stepped forward and cleared his throat. It was clear that he was enjoying his role of matchmaker. He'd dressed up a little himself for the affair by donning his hand-tooled Justin boots and the black tailcoat he'd worn on his own wedding day. Confident in the splendid impression he and his hapless family were making, he began his pitch.

'Well, boys, it's time to start the introducin', so we won't waste time. I'm gonna tell the little lady your names so you can start gettin' acquainted. Since she don't speak the lingo so good, you can show her the kind of man you are by some kind of demonstration of your talents – up to you what it is. Jeb, you're eldest so you go first.'

With a conceited smile on his lips, Jeb stepped forward flexing his considerable biceps. He strode over to a nearby upturned old stump with a kindling axe embedded in it, where the firewood for their stove was chopped. Flinging the axe aside into the dust, he bent down and picked up the large block of timber as though it was no weight at all. He heaved it above his head and turned to the others.

'You see the outhouse at the bottom of the yard yonder? I'll toss this piece of wood past it no problem at all.'

His family peered dubiously at the small shack in question. It was a good fifteen yards away – a long stretch even for someone of Jeb's enormous strength.

The behemoth steadied himself for a few seconds, then ran forward a few paces and released his projectile with an inarticulate yell. Sure enough the great hunk of wood flew past the outhouse and disappeared into the undergrowth beyond. Even used as they were to Jeb's phenomenal ability, his kin were mightily impressed and a ragged but spontaneous round of applause went up. With a self-satisfied smirk on his ugly face, the giant swaggered back to his place. Surely that display would win him this contest?

Next up was Sal. He was carrying a shiningly well-kept Winchester. Indeed, its immaculately maintained appearance was in sharp contrast to the rat-faced scruffiness of its owner.

He selected a couple of twigs from the ground and handed them to his pa.

'Toss these in the air for me, Pa. Do it same time, different directions and hard as you can.'

At a nod of his son's head, Calhoun threw both twigs into the sky as far as he could. Fast as lightning, Sal raised his gun and shot them both in mid-flight so that four pieces of wood returned to earth instead of two. Unlike the vainglorious Jeb, he didn't seek to garner praise for this amazing marksmanship, but immediately afterwards he was studiously checking his weapon for its continued worthiness. But he too was quietly content with his performance and confident that it must have impressed his potential bride.

Last came the turn of the youngest of the litter, the half-idiot Aaron. He stood in the middle of the yard, patted back his flaxen hair, then launched into a rapid series of back flips and somersaults. This truly was an amazing display of acrobatic prowess for, as so often, Nature had compensated for lack of mental ability by a corresponding increase in athletic talent. At the end, he wound up on one knee, his arms spread out for the expected cries of appreciation. Out of rough good humour, his brothers obliged him, though their raucous shouts of encouragement seemed to bear more than a little trace of mockery.

Before he brought these ludicrous proceedings to an end, Calhoun addressed his brood one last time.

'Thank you, boys. I'm sure Miss Isabella is mighty bowled over by that display. But she'll need more time to think things over and get to know you better. Tomorrow me and the stranger are gonna take off for few days – we have a little business to attend to. Profitable business. That'll give you a bit more time to show this here lady just what fine examples of manhood you are. When we get back, there's gonna be a weddin' and, by God, we don't need no preacher-man. I'm gonna marry the happy couple myself!'

The brothers automatically let out a half-hearted cheer of approbation while their minds wrestled with the latest piece of news their old man had unloaded on them. What the devil did their pa want with their other captive? Where could they be going and how much money was involved? However, they knew better than to question their senior too closely and their low minds soon returned to Isabella. They might go along with the old man's plan of a proper courtship and wedding or, on the other hand, they might not. It all depended on what sort of mood they were in or – more exactly – how much whiskey they consumed. The main thing was, whatever his reasons, the old man would be absent and no one could stop them if they decided to give the bride-to-be a try out for the matrimonial couch. Sure, he might raise a ruckus on his return but they all knew that this was what was going to happen anyway. So what if it just happened a little sooner?

As for Calhoun himself, he was well satisfied with the morning's results. He'd thrown off suspicion of his trip with Bill by cleverly using the bait of the woman. Things would go a lot more smoothly on the journey with just him and his prisoner. His boys just seemed to attract trouble wherever they went. If they ran into the posse seeking the Brazos Kid, things would go more easily without their obviously villainous presence. It so happened that he had, stashed away from his own murky past, the handcuffs and star of a deputy he had killed down Oklahoma way. With these accoutrements of the law and the wanted poster of Bill still in his possession, he was sure he could bluff his way through to his destination posing as a lawman delivering his prisoner. Once they got the hidden loot, Bill would be got rid of. Heck, he might even collect the reward money for bringing in the corpse of the infamous Brazos Kid! But that could raise some awkward questions about his own past and might be better avoided. Either way, he was going to return home a rich man and a hero in the eyes of his precious sons. And, he asked himself piously, wasn't that what all loving fathers really cared about?

CHAPTER 14

That night was a nightmarish one for both Bill and Isabella. He was still tied to the chair in the main room of the place while she was incarcerated in the filthy dark hole under the floor, which served as a kind of cellar. The next few hours would not turn out to be comfortable for either of them.

The Calhouns began to drink heavily, both to celebrate the upcoming nuptials and the hoard of cash they hoped would presently come their way. None drank more copiously than the head of the dissolute clan and soon he lay face down on the table, his long hair and tangled beard spread out around him, totally insensible with the effects of drink. Bill had been watching the raucous proceedings all evening with ever-growing anxiety. Lashed tightly in an upright position, it was impossible for him to snatch a wink of sleep. Not that he could have done so anyway with all the riotous commotion going on around him. As the men got drunker and drunker, so did his growing unease. Violent and unpredictable though they were, he didn't fear that they would hurt him, for even they recognized that, for the moment at least, he was their meal ticket; but he was concerned about Isabella. The thin veneer of civilization quickly fell away from types like this after a few drinks and what remained was ugly, base and dangerous. No woman would be safe in the vicinity of these scoundrels once liquor had unleashed their animal instincts.

He'd noticed that Jeb and Sal had seemed to hold back some as their father got more and more inebriated. Now that the old man was out cold on the table and beginning to snore, they withdrew to a corner and began to whisper to one another in conspiratorial fashion. As for Aaron, he merely sat around grinning stupidly to himself. It took only a small amount of alcohol to completely overwhelm a brain as impaired as his; he would play no part in whatever was afoot.

Eventually the urgent whispering ceased and Sal advanced on Bill, unfurling a scarf from his neck. For a horrible moment, Bill feared that he had been wrong and that they were about to kill him after all, and to do it by one of the most unpleasant methods of all – strangulation. He opened his mouth to scream but Sal merely used the opportunity to stuff the scarf into his mouth as a gag. Then he and his partner in crime, Jeb, made their stealthy way toward the trapdoor that opened on to the cellar, all the while keeping a wary eye on their dozing father.

But if they hoped to catch their intended victim off guard, they were sorely mistaken. Alerted by the sounds of rowdy carousing followed by ominous silence overhead, Isabella was prepared for what was to come next. As soon as the trapdoor was lifted, she let out a piercing cry that startled her would-be assailants and stopped them in their tracks. Calhoun roused from his deep slumber and looked blearily around him. His gaze fell on his miscreant sons, frozen comically in the guilty act of raising the trap-door to the cellar, and he rose instantly, angrily toss-ing aside the chair he had been siting on.

'What the . . .' he roared and stormed over to the petrified malefactors. Seizing both men by the lobes of their ears, he dragged them roughly across the floor like a schoolmaster with two errant pupils. Once he got to the door, he kicked it open and propelled both men into the night.

'You can sleep on the porch tonight,' he yelled, flinging a few blankets out after them. 'That'll help cool off your passions!'

Then he stomped in, muttering about rebellious offspring and took the choking gag from Bill's mouth.

'Don't worry none about them boys,' he clucked reassuringly. 'They'll come to their senses once the drink wears off.'

Bill very much doubted that, for meanness and viciousness were ingrained in their nature. Once he and Calhoun left, he shuddered to think of the fate that awaited poor Isabella. The only solution would be to overpower the old mountain man first chance he got and hurry back to save his companion. But in view of the toughness and cunning of the trapper, that would be no easy thing, no easy thing at all.

Early next morning a lone figure emerged from the cabin and, clutching his belly, made his way precipitately towards the outhouse at the end of the yard. It was Aaron, who was feeling the after-effects of the previous night's excesses and was in need of urgent relief. Once inside the smelly edifice that was his destination, he sat himself down with evident relief at having made it in time. After a while, however, he was puzzled to hear a strange, fizzing noise coming from behind him somewhere. It sounded as though it was outside the shed and, as he was in no position to investigate at that particular moment, he just stayed put and listened intently. It was somehow oddly familiar and he racked his brains to figure where he had heard it before. Then, suddenly, he got it: last Fourth of July in Santa Fe. It was the noise that the fireworks made just before they went off. That information had just registered on his befuddled mind, when the stick of dynamite placed against the back of the hut ignited with a deafening roar and blew him and the entire rickety structure to kingdom come.

As the shards of burning timber rained down and smoke billowed through the shattered yard, Jeb emerged from the dusty chaos, peering around in bewildered fury and brandishing a six-shooter in his hand. Wakened suddenly from his uneasy sleep on the rough boards of the porch, he had reacted instinctively and unthinkingly by plunging immediately towards the trouble. It was not a wise move for before he could even clear his blurred vision to sight a target, someone got the drop on him and clinically drilled a lump of lead between his piggy eyes. He pitched forward silently like a tall tree felled by a woodsman's axe and hit the ground in an ungainly sprawl. The arrogant, hectoring bully was no more and, in death, seemed already to be nothing other than a heap of clay, which would gradually settle back into the earth from which it had come.

Wilier than his elder brother and also finding himself bereft of his favourite Winchester, Sal had slipped back into the house and was now looking through one of its narrow windows. He had retrieved his weapon and was ready to use it against whoever or whatever had caused this rude awakening. Pa Calhoun had stationed himself at the other window, Colt pistols in each hand, and ready to do battle with the unknown enemy who had attacked them in such sudden and deadly fashion.

But outside there now reigned an unearthly quiet. Aside from the charred remains of the outhouse, now visible through the clearing haze, and the prone shape of the recently deceased Jeb, it was as if nothing had happened and life was just proceeding along as normal. Calhoun shook his head as if to rid it of this sense of unreality and directed a terse question to his son.

'Where's Aaron?'

Sal hesitated before answering.

'I think he was in the outhouse. He stepped over me on the way out.'

The hardened old villain fought back a bitter tear as he stared out the window. No person is entirely without feelings and even this rough, brutal man rued the loss of his own flesh and blood. But now was not the time to mourn, not while their killer or killers still lurked somewhere in the neighbourhood. Now was the time to preserve his own life and that of his sole remaining son; and to exact vengeance for the dead ones.

'You out there,' he shouted. 'What the hell do you want?'

There was a pause before the reply came back.

'Let the woman go free and I'll leave you alone.'

Calhoun turned to Bill, who was still securely trussed up and had been a helpless witness to all the foregoing excitement. Now was the time to play his part.

'You recognize that voice, Kid?'

'Yeah,' came the answer. 'It's *El Bruto*. He's a member of my gang.'

It flashed through the cowboy's mind that, ever watchful of his mistress, the Mexican had noticed her tampering with the coffee and had only feigned drinking it. He must have trailed them and witnessed their capture. Now he had made his bid to rescue Isabella; but what had he in mind for Bill?

'How come he's only askin' for the woman?'

'Oh, 'cause he's crazy about her and don't want anything else in the world.'

Calhoun shook his head in wonder at this bizarre state of mind. A fortune in cash to be had and the lunatic outside was prepared to risk his life for a mere girl!

'I reckon this jasper's on his own,' he said, turning to Sal. 'Slip out the back and see if you can work your way round.'

With gusto, Sal pumped a fresh cartridge in the magazine of his rifle. He reckoned this would be easy meat. Then, cautiously opening the back door, he darted out into the weeds that grew in profusion around it and instantly disappeared from sight.

There was a long wait after that, or so it seemed to the two men tensely listening in the shack for the sound of gunfire. But when it came, even though they were expecting it, the shock ran through them like a bolt of electricity.

Calhoun craned his neck to get a better view through the window.

'Did you get him, Sal? Is he dead?' he called eagerly.

Once more there was an excruciating delay before the response came at last.

'It is your Sal who is dead. Now perhaps you will

146

give me what I ask.'

The old man gave a groan of despair and sank to the floor, burying his face in his hands. Bill felt almost sorry for him at that moment. In the space of about a quarter of an hour he'd lost all three of his sons – his entire family was now gone. But it was the old man's boundless greed and ruthlessness that had led to their destruction; he was the architect of his own misfortune. Now it was his turn and he would have to face the retribution that he himself would have brought about.

By and by the oldster pulled himself together. He was too much of a fighter to fall to pieces at this stage. His face regained the look of flinty determination that was his habitual expression. He stood up, strode across the floor to the cellar door and flung it open. He descended and shortly after emerged with a struggling, dishevelled Isabella. She and Bill had only time to exchange one fleeting glance of affection before Calhoun thrust her out on to the porch, a gun pointing at her head. Her body effectively shielded that of her captor while his back was to the doorway. There was no way he could be got at without the risk of hurting his hostage.

'You want the woman so bad, *hombre*,' he jeered. 'Come down and get her. If you don't, I'll put a bullet through that pretty head of hers and save us all a lot of trouble.'

The threat was obviously real; the old mountain man was crazy with grief and didn't care about anything at this stage. After a while, *El Bruto* slowly emerged from the bushes at the end of the yard.

'Toss your side-iron away or the girl gets it,' rasped Calhoun.

For only a second *El Bruto* hesitated, then he complied with the order. He knew that this action was probably his death warrant but his love for Isabella surpassed even his instinct for survival. For the last time, with the eyes of a sad, faithful but ultimately rejected pet, he regarded his cherished mistress. He was ready to give up his life for her and she could not but be moved.

Still clutching Isabella tightly, Calhoun took the gun muzzle from her temple and deliberately pointed it at the midriff of his antagonist.

'I'm gonna belly-shoot you, boy. That way you'll die real slow and have plenty of time to think about how you killed all my kin. Say your prayers now, you sonuvabitch; in a while you won't be in no condition to say anything!'

His finger was tightening on the trigger when Isabella threw all her weight against him and knocked him momentarily off balance, spoiling his aim. In fury, he raised his pistol high in the air and drove the butt hard across her scull. As she swooned senselessly to the ground, he turned once more to his opponent to finish the job he had started. But *El Bruto* had seized upon those vital few seconds for a desperate defence; looking around him frantically for the nearest weapon, his eyes lit on the kindling axe that Jeb had discarded the previous day. He now snatched this up and flung it with all his might at his foe, just as the latter was steadying his gun to deliver the fatal shot.

Whether by good luck or good judgement, the blade of the implement struck its target square in the chest. Calhoun dropped to his knees, spouting blood from his wound. The gun dropped from his hand and he stared straight ahead of him as if he already saw the shades of night coming to envelop him. Then he fell forward into the dust, writhed once and lay for ever still.

El Bruto rushed forward and anxiously examined Isabella. She had been knocked unconscious but was still breathing and even stirred a little in his arms. To his relief, she would be all right. At this point he heard Bill call from inside the cabin and the expression on his face turned from solicitude to an altogether different emotion. He walked over to Calhoun's corpse and callously wrenched the axe from his body. Then he entered the shack with a purposeful stride.

When Bill saw the grim expression on *El Bruto*'s ill-favoured countenance, he fell suddenly quiet. It was evident that this was not an ally come to rescue but an enemy come to slay. Perhaps the tool in the Mexican's hand was to cut him loose, but he very much doubted it. It seemed more likely that he was about to share the fate of a certain recently deceased mountain man.

El Bruto crossed the floor in a few rapid strides and raised the axe up to deliver a fatal stroke. Instinctively Bill closed his eyes and shrank back in anticipation of the murderous blow. But instead he heard a gasp like a suddenly deflated balloon and the sound of a something heavy tumbling. Opening his eyes again, he perceived his about-to-be executioner lying stone dead on the floor, the bone handle of a large knife protruding from between his shoulder blades. A dark figure stood in the doorway of the place; evidently this was the one who had just intervened to save his life but, for an instant, Bill could not identify his saviour. Then the man moved into the room towards him and he recognized the familiar features of his long-time guard – Juan. He pulled his weapon from *El Bruto*'s back, casually wiped it off on the dead man's shirt and, without so much as glancing at Bill, he went outside again to tend to the stricken woman on the porch. Despite the cowboy's urgent pleas to be released, Juan made no reply and kept his distance. Evidently he had scouted ahead of the others and was now waiting for Don Alonzo and the main party to arrive. What happened then was up to the volatile bandit chief, who might not have taken too kindly to a gringo making off with his sister. Bill slumped dejectedly in his chair; like a leaf being tossed about by a playful wind, his fate was once again in the air. As usual, all he could do was wait and hope that Lady Luck, who had so far favoured him, would once again come to his aid. But he had used up a lot of his capital of good fortune; now perhaps was the time when he must pay it back.

CHAPTER 15

Sheriff Delaney and his men were close enough to have heard the explosion at the cabin and the subsequent gunshots. The source of the trouble was evident too from the distant plume of smoke that rose from the destroyed building. But, as usual, the seasoned campaigner knew when to exercise caution and not charge directly into a battle without a bit of reconnaissance first.

'You fellers stay here,' he ordered. 'Me and Yellow Dog are goin' to check out what's happening up ahead. We'll report back to you in a little while.'

He didn't get any arguments about this plan. Most of his cowardly followers were not too keen to get caught up in the middle of a firefight. Especially one with dynamite being tossed around.

Delaney and the Indian climbed the steep slope keeping to the cover of dense pine. It was hard, slow going for both man and horse this way but it was safer to make the approach unobserved. They eventually emerged a bit above the site of the mountain men's

lair and gazed down on the scene below. The charred
remains of the outhouse were still smouldering and
nearby lay the inert body of Jeb. That was about all
they could make out from where they were standing.

Delaney turned to Yellow Dog.

'Looks all quiet down there now. I'm gonna investigate. Keep me covered.'

The brave nodded his agreement and the sheriff
got down off his pony to creep soundlessly towards
the cabin. Once he got near, he drew his gun and
advanced carefully into the arena of combat. First he
checked out the giant in the centre of the yard. From
the small, neat hole in the middle of the cadaver's
forehead it was clear that death had been sudden
and instantaneous. Glancing towards the wreckage of
the toilet, Delaney noted that it had been in use at
the time of the blast; a solitary boot with the foot still
intact even now stood among the debris. Probably
the rest of its owner was scattered about nearby, but
Delaney wasn't eager to find out. As he headed
towards the veranda of the cabin, he spied the
defunct outline of Pa Calhoun there, lying face up,
his face distorted by a demonic look of rage and
madness and his chest split open with a gaping
wound. Delaney gagged his mouth as the bile rose in
his throat and he stepped across the body into the
darkness of the gloomy shack. God alone knew what
further horrors awaited there.

As his eyes grew accustomed to the shade, he was
not altogether surprised to see yet another casualty

sprawled out on the floor there. It was what was left of *El Bruto,* his torso soaked in blood and still clutching a gory axe in his hand. Already the flies were starting to crawl over his decomposing flesh. Nearby was a chair festooned with long strips of rawhide; it was empty now but obviously someone had been tied up there. Who and why? And what was the cause of the massacre outside and inside the cabin? The lawman was still puzzling these questions when he heard a shout from Yellow Dog.

'Got another dead man up here in the rocks, Nehemiah. Shot clean through the heart.'

Delaney holstered his revolver and made his way up to the place of this latest discovery. Another mountain man, he pondered when he got there, that made four in all. Plus what he would bet was one of the Brazos Kid's gang. What the devil had happened here? The only thing that made sense was that these local hunters had kidnapped a member of the bandits for ransom or reward, had been tracked down to their hiding-place and summarily dealt with. In that case, the outlaws had to be close, real close. But to persuade his timid deputies to tangle with them would be difficult, especially when he brought them news of this latest batch of killings. He would have to be particular in the way he presented the news to them. One wrong word would likely spook them, but if he put across his own slant on things, he might be able to urge them to one last effort. It would all rest on his powers of persuasion.

When he got back he could see from the expressions on the faces of his men that they were more than a little nervous. Their imaginations had run riot about what lay ahead, aided by some sly suggestions from Travers and O'Flaherty. With a brisk, businesslike air, their chief gathered them around him and commenced his spiel.

'I won't lie to you men, it's a bit of a mess up ahead. There's five men dead and some aren't a pretty sight. Looks like some mountain men went up against the Brazos Kid gang and came off second best. These *hombres* aren't about to give up without a fight.'

He paused to let that sombre reflection sink in. Having got the bad news over with, the cunning oldster continued with his address, this time putting his own devious spin on the situation.

'But the way I see it, we're in a great position. One of the bandits was killed, so they're a man down. Likely some of the rest of the gang got wounded in the shoot-out. Last but not least, they must be wore out from constant runnin' and fightin'. I know you're tired too and keen to get back to your families. But I'm callin' for one last effort. If we hit them now and hit them hard, we could be on our way home this evening – not as empty-handed failures but as heroes and rich men.'

There was a thoughtful silence as the deputies deliberated on the sheriff's words. The danger was great and some were bound to die but if they succeeded, the rewards were equally great. The survivors would be forever feted as the men who brought down the infamous Brazos Kid; they'd become a legend in their own lifetime. Not to mention the small matter of retrieving their own money and collecting the bounty on the Kid's head.

Surprisingly, it was Stu Harker, the most faint-hearted of the lot, who eventually broke the impasse. This was the individual who had so half-heartedly assisted Hal Jenkins to capture Bill in the first place, which had been the start of all the latter's troubles. But many weeks on the trail had wrought a perceptible change in him. His normally well-kept clothes had become dirty and frayed. Instead of being neat and severely plastered down, his hair now stuck out wild and unkempt, while on his chin there had sprung up a thick, grey stubble. The trappings of civilization had fallen away from him and now he was little better than a beast who had scented the closeness of his prey.

'Well, what are we waiting for, fellers?' he said looking around him with a new light of combativeness in his eyes. 'There's a fortune to be made for just one day's work. I don't know about you but I sure ain't gonna miss out.'

The prospect of release from the drudgery of his job as a store clerk along with the added incentive of raising his lowly status in the estimate of the other townsfolk (especially the female kind who routinely ignored him) had quite turned his head. With a wild whoop, he scooped off his hat and whipped it against the rump of his mount, so that the startled animal took off at a breakneck rate.

His companions milled around for a moment or two, regarding one another uncertainly. But if timorous Stu was game for action, it would be quite a stain on their manhood if any of them backed down. So, some more enthusiastically than others, they followed in his wake, with the grimly smiling sheriff bringing up the rear. Thus far, his tactics had worked; now all that remained was the final showdown.

But no amount of glib talk would win him that battle; victory, if it came at all, would have to be purchased with blood and death.

When Don Alonzo and the rest of his gang had arrived at the same scene that Delaney had so lately inspected, the outlaw leader showed little sign of his mood, merely ordering that Bill be freed from the chair he was lashed to and transferred to a horse. With his hands still bound, the cowboy had to stay to the rear of the column of riders in the company of Juan, while Isabella rode up front with her brother. The young lovers had no opportunity to exchange even so much as a word but Bill could see from the worried expression on her face that she was concerned about what Alonzo would do with them. Only when they reached the main track again did the inscrutable hidalgo indicate what way the wind was blowing.

'Bring up the prisoner!' he peremptorily commanded Juan.

157

When Bill was brought before him, he regarded the rancher sternly.

'What excuse do you have for your behaviour?'

At this impudent question, Bill felt the anger that had long been building up in him explode.

'Excuse?' he said through gritted teeth. 'What excuse does a man need to make a try for freedom, when he's been kidnapped and held against his will, tied up day and night, his money stole and his life threatened? Not to mention his reputation for honesty ruined by being forced to take part in criminal activities? Kill me for it if you like but I'll see you in hell before I apologize to you for wanting to get away from all that!'

He stopped, breathing hard and shaking with impotent fury. All the frustration, the heartache of the past several weeks had been released at last. He didn't care if it meant his doom. He was tired of being pushed around like a pawn in the devilish chess game that Don Alonzo was playing with the law. Now was the time to make a stand against the unfair and inhumane way he had been treated.

Don Alonzo showed no reaction to this outburst but merely gazed at him impassively for a moment or two before turning to his sister.

'And you, Isabella, why did you take the side of a stranger against your own kin? Did I wrong you in some way that you have betrayed me thus?'

Isabella looked a little abashed at this reproach but answered in a steady voice.

158

'You did not wrong me, *mi hermano*, but you wronged this man. It was for this injustice that I helped him escape.'

'Really,' relied Alonzo coolly, 'and it wasn't because you are in love with this gringo?'

At this, Isabella dropped her head and blushed violently.

It was answer enough for Don Alonzo and he switched his attention to Bill again.

'And you, *señor*, do you love my sister?'

It was the young cowboy's turn to get embarrassed, but there could be only one reply.

'Yes, I do'

The bandit chief nodded his head sagely.

'It is as I thought. My sister, who could have married into any of the foremost and wealthiest families in Mexico, chooses to throw herself away on a simple, Northern rancher. Women are so illogical . . . but then that is part of their charm.'

His next remark was directed at his closest henchman and came as sweet music to Bill's ears.

'Juan, free our prisoner and return his money. I will not have my sister marry a poor man!'

Juan rode up and severed Bill's bonds with a single slash of his Bowie knife, before thrusting a bulging saddle-bag into his grasp.

Hardly believing his good fortune, Bill exchanged a delighted look with Isabella. To gain his life, liberty and the woman he loved all at once was almost more than he could take on board. Not to mention the small matter of his hard-earned cash! For her part, Isabella seemed equally overwhelmed and was already thanking her brother profusely. But the object of her gratefulness just held up his hand in a gesture of modest denial as he responded to her.

'Please, do not thank me. I do no more than what is right. The happiness of my family is of the utmost importance to me and nothing counts more than that. Even if he is of humble stock, Beel is a noble man at heart. He has shown that many times on our journey together. I am sure he will make you a good match . . . and if there are any children . . . well, just make sure to name one Alonzo. That will be thanks enough.'

Beaming with joy, Bill and Isabella wasted no time in taking their leave. As they cantered away, chatting merrily and excitedly, already making plans for their new future together, Don Alonzo and his group watched them calmly. But they were Mexicans after all, men of a passionate Latin temperament and, for all their toughness and villainy they could not help but be moved by the happiness of these two young sweethearts. So when the couple turned to wave a final farewell, they could restrain themselves no longer. Led by Don Alonzo himself, they grabbed hold of their sombreros and flung them wildly skywards.

'*Viva!*' they shouted. '*Viva* the Brazos Kid!'

The hats were still in the air when Sheriff Delaney and his posse came galloping round the bend. . . .